Before I Lose My Style

Mike Kaspar

SPUNKY BOOKS

Before I Lose My Style
By Mike Kaspar

Published by Spunky Books
West Hollywood, CA
spunkybooks.com

LIBRARY OF CONGRESS CATALOGING-IN-PUBLICA-TION DATA

Kaspar, Mike
Before I Lose My Style/ Mike Kaspar

ISBN 978-0-9794241-5-1
Library of Congress Control Number: 2008907125

FIRST EDITION
2008

for Robert

"It is in the long run essential to the growth of any new and high civilization that small groups of men can escape from their neighbors and from their governments, to go live as they please in the wilderness. A truly isolated, small, and creative society will never again be possible on this planet…"

—From the lecture, "Mankind and the Universe," delivered to the German and Austrian Physical societies by Freeman Dyson. Quoted from John McPhee, *The Curve of Binding Energy*.

"The measure of the intensity of love
Is measure, also, of the verve of earth."

—Wallace Stevens

Before I Lose My Style

1

THIS AUTUMN a pirate radio station has begun broadcasting from somewhere in Silver Lake. They start playing music soon after sundown and are usually still on the air when I fall asleep. Russ mentioned the station to me a few weeks ago, and since then it has become the only thing I listen to in the evenings. Before the illegal station, I usually had my radio set to a jazz station from Long Beach. I'm not really a big jazz fan; I own a large library of CDs, but less than a dozen of them could be classified as jazz. I never go to jazz clubs. I enjoy the music enough, but the main reason I tuned in to the jazz station was the variety. It seemed like the only station in Los Angeles that didn't just play the same twenty songs over and over.

This pirate station plays much of the indie rock loved by me, mixed with music I don't know and overlooked bands from the past. Even a song you've played millions of times becomes a wonderful surprise when you hear it unexpectedly on the radio. Out of context, you never quite recognize the opening chords. For a few seconds you can't quite place them, but they stir pleasant, if ineffable, memories. Yesternight I heard one of the best Yo La Tengo songs sandwiched between Jonathan Richman and a track from *Dusty in Memphis*. The dislocation made the familiar song revelatory.

Tonight the music is mellow electronic tracks, lots of Boards of Canada, it seems. It isn't indie rock, but it feels right at this late hour. I pour myself a glass of water from the pitcher in the fridge. I live on a high floor in a building downtown; on clear nights like this, with all the condo lights off, the hills are sparkling sodium gold. While I drink the water, I look out the condo's windows towards Silver Lake, towards the neighborhood in which somewhere, in some old basement or disused guest house, some anonymous guy is sorting through his favorite discs to choose what next to play and send out to the audience he is not quite sure is there, while, most probably, a van steered by some tired federal agent winds its way among the hills, looking for the source of the transmission, looking to stop the broadcast.

The guy I brought home from the club—excusing myself early from my friends—is asleep behind me on the couch, wearing only the boxers he pulled on after sex, dozing off without any blankets, using an armrest for a pillow.

He is young. Since my boyfriend left last year, this has become a habit. These boys are always over twenty-one (or at least savvy enough to get into clubs underage), so I'm not doing anything wrong. Yet I have at least a decade on most of them. I have my mortgage, my car, my career, my responsibilities—while they are in college, or finishing college, or skipping out on college to work some dead-end job or dead-end Hollywood fantasy. In summary, they're not yet adults.

I'm hardly the first man to pick up guys much younger than him. What shocked my friends—and me as well—was that this constituted a sudden change of behavior. Before my boyfriend, I always dated guys my own age. Then again, before my boyfriend, I was these guys' age. More importantly, while I did have a couple one-night stands and stupid flings before my boyfriend, I did, for the most part, date. I would become friends with guys, go to movies, have conversations over coffee, joke around. Whatever I'm doing now, it isn't dating.

This guy tonight is quite handsome. He is muscular in the way some guys are after playing sports in high school, not in the calculated, bulging way of those of us who go to the gym regularly. A benefit of my expired relationship is a very well-built figure. My boyfriend encouraged me to go to the gym with him after work. As a result, I now find that I can wear a pair of jeans and a well-cut shirt to a club and be fairly certain that some young guy will come up and start flirting with me. I am not a fool. I know that nine out of ten guys in their early twenties are not interested in a guy in his early thirties. But that ten percent can be counted on to be out there. And some of that ten percent is ridiculously hot. I try not to think about their motivations. Whatever their reasons, it keeps me entertained on the weekends.

I DROP THE GUY HOME on my way to brunch with my best friend Travis and his girlfriend. Ron will also be there. Ron asked Travis and me to go to the Getty with him this afternoon because he is auditioning for an all-male production of *Lysistrata* and thinks that looking at ancient art will help him prepare. He is a method actor, he will explain with little provocation.

I generally avoid helping Ron prepare for auditions. Two weeks ago Ron dragged Travis to Medieval Times to prepare his audition for a modern dramatization of *Sir Gawain and the Green Knight.* They did improvisation exercises in Old English during the car ride to Anaheim and back. I can't imagine Travis enjoys such trips. I suspect he is just too nice to say no. Undoubtedly, Ron pushes Travis to go, in preference to the rest of us, because he likes being seen in public with Travis. Ron has a boyfriend named Allan, and I contend it is Allan's responsibility to help Ron with these preparations. I agreed to go to the Getty today because there are certain artworks in Los Angeles I treat like beloved aunts: I visit them regularly and with emotionally charged familiarity. There is a Diebenkorn at LACMA, an underappreciated Van Gogh at the Hammer, so much at the Norton Simon (my favorite), and Cézanne's still life at the Getty.

My dislike of Ron is well known within our group of friends. Ron is the guy who buys a new wardrobe each season and then subtly derides you for continuing to wear your favorite, old shirt. Ron is the guy who demands you go to the new, trendy restaurant no matter how bad the food might be. Ron is the guy who makes sure you know he just went to the new, trendy restaurant if you aren't the one who was lucky enough to accompany him there. Ron keeps you up to date on the furniture he is planning to buy to decorate his and his partner's house. Ron will show you the decorating magazines that told him to buy that furniture. He just happens to have those magazines in his car. He also has digital photographs to show you of the resort he and his boyfriend visited, although the trip was months ago and you already saw photos. Ron is what happens when an unchecked id is merged with a superego constructed from mass market consumer culture. Ron talks a lot. Loudly.

Today we are meeting at a restaurant on La Cienega that I enjoy. I am the last to arrive and find Ron, Travis, and Travis's girlfriend, Denise, already seated and drinking their coffee on the patio. I still don't know Denise very well, so I'm caught off guard when, after ordering, she catches my eye and says, "I heard you fucked a total hottie last night," with a demonic grin.

"I guess Ron got you guys all caught up," I say.

"Yes," she says, "I think he's quite jealous. Was your date really that good looking?"

"He was a USC undergrad, nice enough guy."

"You didn't answer my question." Denise is a lawyer.

"He goes to USC? Is he a friend of Russell's?" asks Ron.

"I didn't ask if he knew Russ. I'd rather avoid the issue. I don't like the idea of messing around with someone a good friend of mine is or was involved with."

"Christ, Damon, you're gay." Denise points at me accusingly with a teaspoon as she says this. "Half the guys you've fucked are probably ex-tricks of friends or ex-tricks of ex-tricks if you took the time to chart it out. Get over it."

All this causes me more anxiety than my friends realize. I'm a professor at an undergraduate university, so it seems inevitable that someday I will run into one of my students at a club. The only thing that has prevented that from happening already is the low enrollment of LGBT students in the physical sciences. I'm out at school, so the gay thing is not a problem. I just worry about the impropriety of socializing with students. My strategy is to simply be open about everything and avoid online dating entirely. The last thing I need is for some Craig's List hookup to turn out to be a student in my lab. Everything was so much easier before my boyfriend left.

Ron suddenly grabs my wrist and places my hand between both of his. He looks meaningfully into my eyes. "I know how hard it can be to readjust to living on your own," he says. He has a surprisingly tight grip. "What you are doing…it isn't healthy. I mean, I know you're careful, it isn't the STD thing I'm talking about. It is your spirit. I have someone I want you to meet. He's a banker. He goes to my Wednesday-night yoga class. You so should come to the class. The yoga would be cleansing for you…you need to exhale your pain before it becomes imprinted on your muscles. And I could also introduce you to this guy." Perhaps it is the yoga that gives Ron so tight a grip.

"It is kind of you," I say, "but I hate being set up."

"This is different, Damon. You need to continue your journey; you need to move on. You'll like this guy. He is like you: healthy, well built, a professional. And Damon, you know me. You know I can see inside people. I can see he is a really good soul."

"Ron," interrupts Travis, "I think Anderson Cooper is seated in the booth across from us."

"Oh my gosh, oh my gosh," Ron releases my hand and turns in his seat to look. "I heard on Oprah that he meditates. You can tell; he's so centered." I mouth the words "thank you" to Travis.

If anyone is being ogled in the restaurant, it is Travis. Simply, he is a beautiful man. We met in college, so I've long grown accustomed to being out with him and having strangers stare at him. The staring has grown more pronounced in the last two years since Travis is on TV now. He majored in art and found he liked sculpture and woodworking. He focused on furniture making after graduation, doing finish-carpentry jobs to keep himself afloat. After I got my job, I hired him to do work in my condo to get him some cash. He then became a carpenter on a home-design cable show called *Redecorating Rooms*, on which neighbors refurbish each others homes over a weekend. Travis is now a bona fide minor celebrity. Travis and I dated for about a week in college, but it never got past kissing. He has stuck to girls pretty much since then, without having any lasting relationships.

Ron quickly discovers that the silver-haired man across the restaurant isn't Anderson Cooper, and he and Denise begin arguing if Anderson does indeed meditate or if, as Denise believes, he once worked for the CIA. The topic of my sex life is forgotten and doesn't resurface for the rest of the meal. Denise has to work in the afternoon, so she isn't going to the museum with us. I am surprised after the meal when she gives Travis a kiss on the cheek and asks me to walk her to her car. She is parked around the corner on a side street.

"Damon, I don't know that you have my number." She hands me her card. I reflexively take mine out of my wallet to give to her. "I've gotten along with you these couple of times we've hung out. When Travis and I break up, I'd hate to lose touch with you. We both live downtown; we should have drinks. You know Travis. He wouldn't care if we hung out."

"You guys are breaking up?"

"I've been dating forever, and I still manage to hook up with the gay guys. I should know better by now."

"But Travis isn't gay."

"Look, I'm not putting you in a position. Travis and I talked about this. I already told him I want to remain friends with you. I am not having some drama break up where everyone takes sides. I gotta go. Give me a call. Ciao."

She starts the engine, guns it, but stops about ten yards down the street. She opens her window and yells at me.

"Quick question. I'm just curious. That ex-boyfriend of yours, he really just up and moved out, never giving you a reason it ended? That's what Travis told me."

I walk over to her car so that everybody at the nearby newsstand doesn't hear the details of my failed relationship.

"Yes," I nod, "that sounds about right."

"After being with you since you were twenty-five?"

"Twenty-three," I say.

"Bastard. I mean, I'm sure you're no fucking saint yourself, but that is fucking crap. Don't listen to that twat back there. You earned a free pass to go through whatever you need. Next time he tries to drag you to a yoga class to meet some quality guy, tell him to stick it up his cunt."

Then she speeds away. I rejoin Travis and Ron at my car and I drive us to the Getty. As soon as the tram doors open, Ron rushes to the antiquities collection, temporarily here while the old villa in Malibu is being remodeled. Travis and I will meet Ron in the antiquities after we walk around the gardens. It is late afternoon; if we wait until after going through the galleries, it will be too late to see the grounds. We start at the top of the stream and take the zigzagging path that crosses the stream repeatedly before the water cascades down to the central garden's sunken pond. The trees have lost their leaves; the unlikely equilibrium between riparian grove and drainage ditch that makes this part of the garden compelling is shifted too far toward the latter. Similarly, at the bottom of the path the bougainvillea trellises look too skeletal without the vines' shock of blossoms. The contents of the beds circling the sunken pond has shifted: the hypersaturated cottage garden of a few months ago has withered into a few pale yellow trumpet vines and dormant shrubbery. We don't linger.

The cactus garden alone is unchanged with the season. You

can not walk through the cactus garden but can only look down on it from a balustrade a few floors above. The garden is planted atop a granite rampart that extends some fifty feet outward from the museum in the shape of lower-case "q." We lean on the railing. I look at the horizon, and Travis stares at the cacti. The basin is defined by the high points that surround it—the spires of downtown to the left, the observatory, this hilltop museum, the Palos Verdes Peninsula. Behind PV, the top of Catalina echoes the peninsula. In the ancient world, signal fires on such peaks could communicate great victories or pleas for assistance. If I set a fire atop my building downtown, this distress call could be relayed across the channel to Catalina. Why would I signal the island for help? Maybe the bison. Maybe the buffalo will come to my aid when Al-Qaeda decides to blow up downtown.

"Damon, I wanted to ask you a favor," says Travis. "I just got this email from my cousin. These four musicians he knows are coming to Los Angeles next month. They are a string quartet from Budapest. They are going to be in residence at some music school downtown for a couple of months. I don't know much more than that. I'm not even sure how my cousin knows them. Anyway, he asked me if I'd hang out with them when they get here. Make them feel welcome in town. I figured I'd have them over for dinner."

There are multiple things wrong with Travis's plan. He just purchased a loft and owns no furniture. He might also be one of the worst cooks ever. When I bring up both these issues, he reminds me that Lucinda and I are taking him shopping for furniture next weekend.

"Why don't we just go to a restaurant?" I say. "It would be easier than cooking."

"They came across an ocean. It is the hospitable thing to do. I'll cook something simple."

"No. No cooking for you. Your purgatorial vegan gruel is terrifying."

"I'm a vegetarian right now, not a vegan. And I'd be open to food advice."

I agree to help out.

"I didn't want to bring it up in front of Ron," says Travis. "I don't know anything about these people. I figured a small dinner would be safe. I'll just invite you, Lucinda, and Seth."

We look down at the cactus garden for a while. Tourists come and go. A couple asks me to take their picture with the skyline as a backdrop.

When we're alone again, Travis says, "I really missed you and Lucinda being on the road so much this year. I know you've had a rough time. I wish I could have been here more."

"Thanks," I say, "but the way your career has taken off—of course you had to be away."

"I remember being over at their house when she went into this analysis of these gardens," says Travis. Lucinda is a landscape architect.

I was there, too. I can do a good impression of Lucinda, and I remember parts of the conversation. "The key to the cactus garden

19

is the repetition of shapes," I say. "All cacti of the same type are placed together in cacti domains so the repetition of shapes makes an abstract pattern, like wallpaper or fabric. And something about subtle modulations of color. A little bit of maroon in those beaver-tail things on the far side, a little yellow streaking in the leaves of those agave-looking things and in the needles of the barrel cactus."

"And something about the slightly lavender stone," adds Travis.

"Yes," I bite my upper lip slightly and look sideways, imitating the face Lucinda makes whenever she is considering something carefully. This makes Travis laugh. "It is all about counterpoint. The jaggedness of the rock contrasts with the fleshiness of the cactus, and the lavender color contrasts with the green of the plants."

"I think Lucinda was wrong," says Travis when we stop laughing. "The garden is compelling because it is outside your reach. Like the flooded labyrinth in the central garden. You are separated from it and can never be a part of it. It allows nothing but contemplation."

Sometimes Travis just seems to implode. I suggest we go and find Ron.

When we find Ron, he appears to be working his way around the collection, mimicking the statues and the figures painted on the pottery. He gives but a small nod to acknowledge us. The message is clear: he wants us to leave him alone while he finishes his study. He is standing with one arm extended outward, mirroring a marble statue of Leda lifting off her robe to show a swan that has buried its head between her breasts. Ron moves his knee forward as if he was cradling a swan against his pelvis. Thankfully, the gallery is almost deserted, and the guard has concluded that Ron is harmless.

"I am really envious of Ron's abandon," whispers Travis. "I want to work on my sculpture during this break from the show, but when I sit down to start, it feels like there is nothing in me. I wish I could just throw myself at things the way Ron does."

Travis and I walk along the displays: a man steers a chariot drawn by four rearing horses, a satyr falls to one knee and drinks from a horn, a warrior sinks a spear into a beast's belly. Before a cup decorated with an older man bending down to kiss a half naked adolescent boy, Travis looks at me accusingly and giggles a bit. There is a wreath of golden flowers and leaves, and Travis remarks how inconceivable it would have been for the artisan to consider that this wreath would end up on a hilltop above Brentwood and not in the underworld. Two gryphons devour the flesh of a dying deer, a man with wings on his back and ankles dances atop waves, and a plump bird with a woman's head extends a block and a sphere with arms articulated below her wings.

I stop before a small bronze statue, half a foot tall, of a nude athlete. The right arm is broken at the shoulder, and the legs end at the kneecap. His left hand rests on his hip, and his right buttock is shifted slightly outward so a curve is formed starting at his chest, moving inward at his waist, and then outward at his full ass and thigh. His eyes are large; his lips, full and tranquil. His bulging upper pecs suggest the power of his chest, and a shallow line snakes up

21

from his belly button, dividing his trunk in half, until it reaches the point where his clavicles meet at the base of the neck. Words cut along the side of his body literally make his flesh into text.

"My gosh," says Travis. I haven't noticed he is standing beside me, as enthralled as I am. We are stunned into silence for several minutes. Had I ever met such a man? No. If I ever met a figure like that, I would follow him wherever he took me.

I do make it upstairs to view the Cézanne before we leave, but I don't really see the painting. I am still dazzled from the statue.

2

THE NEXT SATURDAY MORNING I am to pick up Travis by 10:00, so we can drive to Lucinda and Seth's house in the South Bay and go shopping to furnish Travis's new loft. My day has become more complex because of the boy I picked up at Akbar last night and agreed to take home to West Hollywood. Also, our friends Johnny and CJ are arriving at LAX at 7:00 tonight rather than Tuesday night, and I agreed to pick them up. CJ works as the makeup artist and stylist for *Surf/Trek*, a cable travel series that follows surfers all over the world. Due to an unexpected series of Atlantic storms kicking up some especially high surf, *Surf/Trek* is set to begin filming in Fuerteventura a week earlier than originally scheduled. The boys have to come home early from a vacation in Tokyo, so CJ can turn around and fly out to the Canary Islands the next day. Before CJ started on *Surf/Trek* I would never have guessed a show about surfers needed a makeup artist. Between Travis and CJ, my knowledge of basic cable television has increased extensively over the last couple of years.

Travis is an early riser, so I call him at 8:00 to ask if I can pick him up at 9:30 and make a detour through WeHo. Travis does not care, but getting my drowsy and dragging date washed, dressed, and into my car at this hour proves difficult. Luckily, he is a fan of *Redecorating Rooms,* and the whole ride from downtown to WeHo is taken up by Travis—patiently, seriously—answering the same dozen questions he is repeatedly asked by the show's fans. Many of those dozen questions hinge on which designers are gay and available. When the questioning fan is a woman, these questions switch to which designers are straight and available. Travis is all diplomacy.

Once the boy is dropped off, we jump on the 405 towards Lomita. I try to talk to Travis about furniture for the loft, but he has little to say. He decides the color scheme should be all blacks and grays, so he doesn't have to give it much thought. Everything will naturally match. This monochromatic palette, incidentally, would also be how Travis would dress for the show, had the producers not outlined the style he needs to maintain. Lucinda and I termed the style they've imposed "hipster-fratboy." We take him out shopping at the beginning of each season. Now T-shirts advertising minor-league baseball teams from across the nation and subtly retro polo shirts are sent to him by fanboys and housewives. Our shopping has been reduced to a couple pairs of cargo shorts and work boots, maybe some thermal tops and Henleys to layer under the T-shirts if it gets cold.

The fact that Travis, surrounded by designers who adore

him and expertly qualified to make custom furniture for himself if he were motivated, needs his two best friends, one a scientist and the other a landscape architect, to furnish his new loft has been a great source of amusement among our circle of friends since the time it became apparent that without our assistance the loft would contain nothing more than a pile of blankets and pillows in one corner for sleeping, a cup for drinking water from the faucet, a bowl with chopsticks for his tofu and raw-vegetable creations, and a large pile of books. Travis will explain the dangers of material possessions in a logical, learned manner. Lucinda and I told him if he has a loft in which he plans to invite people over for dinner—say, the stray Hungarian string quartet—philosophically sound or not, he needs a table and chairs to sit on. After that discussion he even faked interest in buying a bed.

Travis and I were roommates our senior year of college, until he bought a pickup with a cab on the back and figured it made no sense to have both an apartment and a truck with room enough in the back for his futon. He moved out and lived in his truck. He drove around the city and parked wherever he felt like sleeping, using the campus gym to shower and pissing in an empty Gatorade bottle that he disposed of each morning. I had to find a new person to sublet the room, and Travis has been itinerant ever since.

The purchase of the loft—which is a loft in the industrial-cavernous, cement-floored, freight-elevatored sense of an artist's loft rather than the posh reworking that has become the center of downtown's newly gentrified real estate market—was Travis's realization that the significant money he was making from *Redecorating Rooms* would not continue indefinitely. He has the opportunity to secure a permanent space to create his art with the large square footage his works demand. He sees the loft as a workspace. I wonder if we will be choking on sawdust and lacquer fumes whenever we visit him.

At the house in Lomita, Lucinda opens the door with a cell phone at her ear. Her expression is serious. She tells the person on the phone that Travis and I have arrived; presumably it is friend rather than a client. She tells us to grab some coffee and muffins from the kitchen and join Seth in the backyard. She promises to be off the phone soon.

Seth greets Travis and me when we walk out on the deck. Seth is a cyclist. He has a truing stand set up on the patio table and is fixing the rear wheel of one of his many bicycles. He goes back to truing the wheel as he talks to Travis and me. With a quick turn of his left hand, he tightens or loosens spokes with a spoke wrench. While he does this, he slowly rotates the wheel with his right hand and watches the distance between the rim of the rotating wheel and the calipers built into the truing stand. This measures the wheel's circularity. He talks to Travis and me in the slow, easy drawl of a surfer, never letting his keen focus wander away from the bicycle wheel.

Besides the cat Lucinda brought into the marriage, Seth and Lucinda have two vizslas, lithe and honey colored, who come scudding across the yard. They are intensely territorial dogs, but right now they only want to play, since they've known me since they were puppies. I wrestle with them on the lawn while Travis wipes the dust off a patio chair and joins Seth at the table.

Seth grew up on this property, which his grandfather purchased when Lomita was all avocado groves. A parcel this size would now be almost impossible to buy in the basin. Large lots like this are subdivided and replaced with cul-de-sacs of cloned duplexes, the side yards hardly wide enough for the sunlight to reach the cement walks between buildings.

The dogs see a squirrel and lose interest in me. I lie back on the grass and look up at the winter-blue sky through a jacaranda's lacy foliage. The backyard looks like it belongs in *Sunset* magazine: deck under the arbor, gas grill, hedges along the property line, pool and hot tub, glazed pots everywhere planted with herbs and ornamental grasses, raised beds hidden in the back for summer vegetables, a row of crape myrtles along the garage. It all seems so distant from my urban existence. When will I ever have the opportunity to recline on my own lawn and gaze at the sky? I understand why Lucinda moved to this sleepy suburb, even if she occasionally threatens to go insane if she designs one more garden for a faux-Mediterranean estate in Palos Verdes. I get up, sit at the table with Seth and Travis, and start drinking my coffee.

"How's the training going?" I ask Seth. I used to go riding with him occasionally, but he has started training seriously for centuries. Now his rides are too long and too strenuous for me to tag along.

"I got in a bit of a wreck," says Seth. He puts down the spoke wrench and rolls up his pant leg and sleeve to show me road rash dressed with 2nd Skin on both his elbow and his knee. "I'm all scratched up on the left side of my body. Lucinda is still mad about it; she is sure I'm going to kill myself one day. I landed on my head and cracked my helmet. The bike is fine except for this slightly tweaked front wheel."

"Was it a car?" asks Travis.

"Yes and no," Seth chuckles. "It was definitely precipitated by a car. Some guy ran a stop sign and made a left in front of me. I had no stop in my direction, so I totally had the right of way. I kept my head about me, did a little evasive maneuvering, veered to the right, and would have been fine. Then, as soon as I realized I was safe, I lost my shit, got really angry, and decided to chase down the driver and tell him off. In my anger I turned too fast and lost control. The rage always gets you. I should know that by now."

Seth goes back to truing the wheel.

"Who is Lucinda talking to?" I ask.

"Allan, for about an hour. She is agitated about something."

Seth heads the crew that implements Lucinda's designs—a sort of in-home contractor: laying sprinklers, pouring cement, planting lawns and flowerbeds. Lucinda herself admits he possesses a touch for growing plants she lacks. He can stroll the neighborhood, discreetly snake a clipping from someone's yard, and within a year grow that clipping into a bush that eclipses the mother plant. The sprawling wisteria that covers the arbor under which we are sitting started as a sprig stolen from the mission in San Gabriel and transported home in a moist paper towel jammed into the bottom of a Styrofoam cup. The generations of Christmas cacti planted in pots around the deck arose from Seth's propagation from a single ancestor plant.

Lucinda exits the French doors as she says good-bye to Allan. She sits. When Lucinda is shaken by something she stops talking like a human and sounds more like an old-school radio broadcaster reading from copy: "Allan has decided he wants to spend the rest of his life with Ron; they're going to have a commitment ceremony. I'm uncertain what is bothering me more: the fact that Allan seems like the least likely member of our group to want to get married—so this decision just feels contrary to his character—or the fact that he wants to get married to Ron in particular. I have tried to like Ron, but in the back of my head I was just counting on Allan to get rid of him someday. This appears unlikely now."

We are shocked. I say, "Are you sure this is really what he wants and not just something Ron is pressuring him into? That has to be it."

"No, Damon, he really wants this."

"The guy is impossible," I say.

"Damon, we've talked about this a million times," says Lucinda.

"Look," says Seth, "when you say this is out of character for him, Luce, maybe—how can I say this—maybe it is out of character with who he used to be. Maybe you are not updating your image of him. He's had the biggest shakeup imaginable in his life since he was diagnosed HIV positive. In the last couple years he has bought a home and put his party days behind him. This marriage thing is consistent with who he has become. Anyway, we just need to give him space and let him to do what he wants. More will be revealed."

"Don't think I'm agreeing with you, Seth, but he is our friend, we love him, we will put up with whomever he decides to love, and we'll smile at his commitment ceremony."

"But why does he want a commitment ceremony?" I ask.

"He's a conservative guy at heart," says Lucinda, "Maybe he thinks it will help legitimize his relationship. But he never said that explicitly. You know how those conservative queers can be. Either it is all about transgressing the ideal in sex clubs and back-room anonymous hookups or it is all about embracing the ideal in cookie-cutter homemaker hell."

"That's what I was saying," said Seth, "that his priorities are different now. He has changed from transgression to embrace-ession."

"That is so not what you said. And embrace-ession is not a word. I'm saying he's always led a split life. He is now favoring one side of the split over the other," says Lucinda.

To an outside observer, Seth and Lucinda always agree on any issue. For them, however, it seems necessary to find some fine distinction between their views that they can bicker about. Whether Allan has always lead a split life and is now favoring one side over another, or whether he has fundamentally changed, seems like the same thing to me. Out of respect, I give Seth and Lucinda a few minutes to argue before I redirect the conversation towards a more fundamental point: how Allan loving Ron is simply not possible. I explain how love and Ron can not even be in the same sentence. I explain the ridiculousness of anyone wanting to spend the rest of their lives with Ron. After some time Lucida politely tells me to stop talking and to keep my mouth busy eating another muffin.

"We all know that Allan's sex life has always been extreme by our standards," says Lucinda. He never talks about it directly, at least to me. I wish he would be more open, because the images I get in my head are probably a lot worse than the truth."

The three of us guys nod in agreement. I'm quite certain I know more than anybody else, since Allan and my ex-boyfriend have been friends since high school. Naturally, my ex-boyfriend filled me in about Allan's fetishes when we were together. Allan's friendship with my ex-boyfriend has caused a lot of discord between the two of us since the breakup; it is only because of shared friends like Lucinda and CJ that Allan and I still speak to one another.

Lucinda continues, "And if it weren't for Ron—who we need to remember is not a bad or evil person, just an annoying one—Allan could probably be putting himself in sketchy situations again with rent boys or midnight strolls in Griffith Park or sex clubs. Whatever Allan's hunger, Ron seems to fulfill it."

"But someone that quenches your kinks isn't love," I say.

"Maybe it is to Allan," says Lucinda.

"I fucked another teenybopper last night, but I don't think

for a moment that I love him."

"Maybe that isn't a distinction Allan makes." She takes a sip of her coffee and sits back in her chair. "I know, Damon, this doesn't sit well with me either, but it isn't going away."

Seth asks when this all is going to take place, and Lucinda thinks they might try to have the ceremony next fall.

"Ron is not nearly as bad as you make him out to be…" begins Travis. I throw a half eaten muffin at him before he can finish whatever enlightened comment he was about to make. The dogs jump all over him to devour the muffin scraps that have fallen in his lap and under his chair. He isn't nearly as uncomfortable as I thought he would be being stuck between the two ravenous animals.

Seth suggests we leave for the furniture store, so we pile into Seth's utility vehicle, one of the few SUVs in Los Angeles that actually does haul plants and tools. We continue the conversation during the drive.

Walking into the showroom, it is obvious why Lucinda chose this store. We know we need modern furniture for the loft, but Travis would never agree to an expensive boutique on Melrose. This store is like a slicked-up IKEA: the furniture wouldn't look out of place in a Swiss airport terminal or a stylish sushi bar, and the prices are still low enough to keep Travis from fleeing.

The company is British owned, so Seth starts talking like Damon Albarn as soon as we enter the store, asking questions about how the fabric on the couches holds up to lager and curry stains and babbling about blokes and birds and stuff. Travis, of course, is recognized by the two employees, and Seth claims he is Travis's agent. The employees dote on Travis and his agent and lead the two around the store.

Lucinda grabs my elbow. "Apparently my husband is in one of his outgoing moods today," she says. "Let's capitalize on their distraction. C'mon, love, we've got work to do."

Some of the armchairs look a little like they belong in the Jetsons' space apartment, but these pieces are the outliers; almost everything is tasteful. We quickly find a dining table, a couch, an armchair, and a coffee table we think will work in Travis's loft. We also find a platform bed with small, built-in nightstands. Rather than a full headboard, there are two smaller backrests on both sides of the bed.

"Those are perfect for reading in bed," says Lucinda, "without being some big, overwhelming wall of wood." She sits on the bed, props some pillows against the backrest, pushes off her shoes (a smart pair of Steve Maddens), puts her feet up on the bed and sits back against the pillows. I walk around to the opposite side and do the same.

"What must we look like?" I say. "Some couple pretending our relationship isn't as far gone as it is, reading the evening paper and a current best seller to distract ourselves from the fact we are no longer having sex."

"Or some girl that doesn't realize she is married to a homo," she says. We laugh. "This would be great for Travis. These nightstand things are awesome. He really should get the king size, considering the scale of the studio. The queen would just look too small."

"Are you worried that if Travis gets all of his furniture in the same place it will just look like he is living in a showroom? Shouldn't he mix it up a bit?" I say.

"He should. But he won't."

"So I've given it some thought. I'm definitely not going to Allan and Ron's commitment ceremony."

"You've given it some thought?" says Lucinda sarcastically. "When, Damon? Was that on the ride over here or when we were looking at couches?"

"I'm serious."

Don't even think about this for a while. It is months off. You're not even allowed to talk about it anymore for a week."

"But I really think…"

"Hush."

"OK, let's talk about something else. Something else I was meaning to bring up. I got you guys' Christmas card this week."

Lucinda looks at me defensively.

I continue, "I found it—not the card itself, mind you, but the letter you included—I found it wildly eccentric."

"Clients only got the card; the letter was for family and friends."

"That doesn't make it any less eccentric," I say.

"Eccentric, I think not. That was useful information, a real gift, not some hokey, fake holiday cheer."

"You and Seth are dangerous when you get together on a

project," I say.

Seth and Lucinda's Christmas card was of tasteful design and message, appropriate for a landscape architecture firm to send to its clients. The letter I found so strange read as follows:

November 2003
Dear Friend,

The following is our Christmas letter, probably a little different than most. This letter may save somebody else's life or your own! The message is simple but medically sound.

Could it be a stroke?

You are enjoying your family's holiday party when great uncle Tibor starts acting even stranger than usual. Was there too much brandy in his eggnog, or could it be a stroke? The symptoms of stroke can be difficult to recognize, but not if you remember these three requests:

1. *Please smile!*
2. *Please put your hands up!*
3. *Please repeat this simple phrase, (insert simple phrase)!*

If uncle Tibor can't comply, call 911 and relate the situation to them. Memorizing these three requests—please smile, put your hands up, and repeat this simple phrase—can save Tibor from serious brain damage. Even amateurs can use these prompts to recognize weakness in the face and limbs and problems speaking that often accompany a stroke.

Could it be a heart attack?

On a bright, warm afternoon you can't believe you are lucky enough to be the only person on the beach. You couldn't be happier sunning yourself in a secluded cove when it happens—a sharp pain in your chest that radiates up your arm and neck. You call 911. (Thank goodness your cell gets reception.) Can you stay alive long enough for the paramedics to find you?

You can administer CPR to yourself by taking as deep a breath as possible and then coughing hard—like you are hacking up a loogie. Do this over and over, every two seconds. Coughing compresses the heart to circulate blood; the deep breaths give you much-needed oxygen. This technique can keep you conscious until help arrives.

love,

Seth and Lucinda

"It may be good advice, Lucinda, that's not what I am quarreling with," I say.

"Useful information is a more valuable gift than any ornate object."

"True, but I'm talking about the context. Do strokes and heart attacks really belong in a Christmas card?"

"Damon, do you really need more saccharine elves and snowmen?"

After knowing her for so long, I think Lucinda's success as a landscape architect arises not only from her formidable portfolio but from her demeanor—her ability to express great energy without ever raising her voice, talking excitedly, moving abruptly, or letting her serene gaze waver. Even in heels and a silk dress with her hair drawn back, I'm sure most clients in initial meetings wouldn't flinch if she were to go outside, grab a spade, uproot their old yard, and begin implementing her vision single-handedly, without ever bothering to draw up a design or change into flats.

So, in truth, sitting on this bed, spatting playfully about her Christmas card, we look less like the neutered couples we were envisioning earlier and more like two old confidants, seducing one another in salacious whispers.

"Maybe you could disseminate this information at a better moment," I say. "Maybe a New Year's card. For you guys, maybe an Arbor Day card. You are all about trees, after all."

"Who has time for that? Christmas cards are tough enough. And Arbor Day? Are you kidding me? Look, I think we got the furniture figured out. Let's get our guy and run it all by him. I'll be the designer and you are his personal assistant. That should round out the entourage."

"Why am I the lowly assistant?" I whine.

"You think you could be the designer, little boy?" she asks as we get out of bed.

I DRIVE TO LAX, and Seth and Lucinda take Travis back downtown after the four of us eat an early dinner. The furniture had to be divided between the SUV and Lucinda's car. I plan to meet up with them after the airport to see if they need any help assembling the pieces.

CJ calls me when he and Johnny clear customs. Sometimes CJ is a girl, and sometimes CJ is a boy. One never knows in advance what gender CJ will choose on a given day. I try to avoid pronouns when talking about CJ in the future tense. Rather than say, "I will pick *him* up at the airport," or "I will pick *her* up at the airport," it is preferable to stick with "I will pick *CJ* up at the airport."

She and Johnny are waiting for me at the curb when I reach the airport. CJ is wearing a smart skirt suit with a bright silk scarf tied around her neck. She not only decided to travel as a girl, but a conspicuously stylish one at that. Johnny hates flying and self-medicates with red wine and Vicodin. He is draped over the pile of suitcases, laughing hysterically. CJ and I push Johnny into the backseat, and we put the suitcases in the trunk. I'm afraid Johnny might open the doors while the car is moving and fall out onto the freeway, so I engage the child safety locks, ensuring that the back doors cannot be opened from the inside.

"Girl," says CJ as we leave the airport, "thank you again for picking us up. I can't believe she got us banned from SuperShuttle. You think a Mary could hold her cocktails and painkillers. I don't know why she raised such a stink when I tried to hire a town car. The rich are frugal about the weirdest shit. I was even paying for it with my own money."

Johnny is shrieking and rolling around my backseat, but we

38

just talk over him.

"CJ," I ask, "isn't it easier to clear immigration when your gender matches the one on your passport?"

"This is my salute to the golden age of travel. Once upon a time stewardesses looked this grand; I thought I would remind them how it is done. And if George Bush and his goons have a problem with fashion, they can stick my wig up their ass. Since those bitches started going fascist at the airport, I make it an issue to look as fabulous as possible when I fly. Fuck all of them."

"Did you guys really get to see Pickle while you were there?" I ask.

"We wired him the money, and he got a flight or a camel ride or whatever and met us in Japan. Damn, that bitch looks fabulous— all lean and glowing and shit. We all need to go on the Peace Corps training regimen."

Pickle is a friend of ours serving in the Peace Corps in Ulaanbaatar, Mongolia's capital. This was the first time in a year he has gotten to leave the country. Johnny paid for Pickle's trip to Japan for him. Pickle's stipend is in the Mongolian currency, so travel even in China is prohibitively expensive. Pickle has email access from the office he works in and sends out tons of mass emails with photos attached to keep us up to date on his service.

"Damon, you won't believe this. I was bored in the airport waiting for the plane so I got on one of those coin-operated Internet terminals and checked the theme for next month's Drag Strip. It's the floating world! It is in three weeks, don't forget. I'll be back by then. Can you believe the luck? I already picked out kimonos for everybody, and now we get a chance to wear them in public. We'll be a whole bathhouse of geishas. I know you're difficult about the drag thing. We'll work out something samurai-inspired for you. It will all be just a Hokusai print come to life in Echo Park.

CJ recounts more of his travels in Japan. Finally, I can't keep quiet any longer and tell him about Allan and Ron and the plans for a commitment ceremony. Johnny's wailing has mellowed to incomprehensible muttering. He will sleep soon.

"You are livid, Mary! Nails! Nails!" says CJ.

"I can't believe they are doing this. I can't stand the little fuck."

"You are too nice. I can deal with the bitch because I tell him off to his face when he pisses me off. Say your piece and just be done. Be done. Are you afraid of offending him? Who the fuck cares? She's dense as fuck anyway."

"You and Johnny have been together a lot longer than them. You ever consider one of these things?"

"No ceremony and crappy dress is going to make my love for Johnny any deeper. Maybe if we got a tax break like the heteros, it would be worthwhile. Actually, if that were true, I'm certain Johnny would demand we tie the knot. After making me sign a prenup. Anyway, no sanction from the government is going to change the nature of our commitment. Besides, what would I do then? Would I be expected to start acting like a wife? Quit work and go to the spa every day and gossip with the society bitches about Botox and

Pilates? Sip martinis in a bubble bath? Hell, I keep working to get time away from that crazy fool. And getting to travel the globe with hotties in swimsuits doesn't exactly sour the deal either. I don't need a ring on my finger to complicate my life even further."

I pull up to their house in Silver Lake and help CJ get Johnny and the luggage inside.

"Fuck," she says after putting down the last suitcase. "You know how much I love that fool. You know what I was trying to say about traveling for my job. I don't do it to get away from him." I almost think CJ is going to cry. "I'm sorry about being all over the top and queeny beyond limits and all PMS-ing tonight. Then you get me all talking about relationships and shit and I just act like I'm sitting on the couch next to Barbara Walters and can let any old shit fly out my mouth."

"Long flights really fuck with you."

"I think it was a week and a half of working hard at not being the loud, ugly American in a reserved society. And fuck, I'm flying out again tomorrow night."

She gives me a big hug and disappears back into the bedroom to check on Johnny.

3

I SPRING FROM MY BED EXCITEDLY THURSDAY MORNING despite a fitful night's sleep. I submitted a grant proposal to the NSF yesterday—less than an hour before the midnight deadline—which I had spent weeks writing. I should have come home and collapsed into a dark slumber, but my mind was too full of equations, still debating what figures could be cut from the overly long proposal without obscuring my logic, still double-checking the proposed budget, that I don't think I slept deeply all night. None of this mental activity quite reached the fanciful abandon of dreams, yet it wasn't conscious thought either, more like my brain relentlessly restructuring itself to best accommodate all the new information I had just finished stuffing it with. My body certainly slept, but I don't think my mind ever did.

I gave myself today off. This semester I don't teach classes on Thursday. A free day when the rest of the world works: how could I not feel cheerful? How could I not see the day as a romp, a reprieve, as found money? I don't shower but cover my tousled hair with a baseball cap and head downstairs to the café across the street. I can make better coffee with the French press in my kitchen, and their pastries are dry, and my couch is more comfortable than their steel chairs wobbling on an uneven sidewalk; but the café gives a view of the businesspeople, clipping by purposefully and yelling into their cell phones, and I can sit in my sweatpants and feel for a day removed from the system.

The man who was behind me in line is waiting to cross the street; he holds his necktie against his chest with his free hand and leans forward slightly as he takes a drink from the narrow hole in the plastic lid that covers his coffee. I am thankful for my mug. I am thankful I can smell the coffee I am drinking.

Days like this make me feel like an undergraduate again: cutting classes, sitting on the quad, half reading and half waiting for someone to walk by and start a conversation, often a friend but sometimes someone you've never shared a word with before—you just recognize one another from numerous classes you've shared or have smiled at each other across the room at a crowded party. How effortlessly chance meetings can lead to acquaintances and acquaintances to friendships with the facile openness of college.

I have no errands that need to be done today.

I abruptly decide to eat lunch at the Curry House. I will finally face this. I will walk into the seat of memory, I will eat a late lunch, and I will emerge with the spell broken. The Curry House will no longer be a charmed locale but just a restaurant where I like the food and can go whenever I want. My first date with my boyfriend was at the Curry House, and we dined there often afterwards. It was our fallback restaurant when we wanted to go out but didn't have the time to make a reservation or the energy to get dressed up or the imagination to think of somewhere else to go. I've avoided the place since the breakup. All that will end today.

Here is what the day will be: I will return to my apartment and eat one hardboiled egg with a dash of salt and a banana. This muffin is not filling enough. The egg and banana should get me through my workout. I will need to change out of these sweatpants because they will not match the red Fred Perry track jacket I will wear to walk to the gym. I bought it at the Fred Perry store in Manchester when I was in England for a conference. The jacket will look good over the white tank top I want to wear to the gym. I will wear my khaki shorts and my New Balances.

I alternate between shoes, because I think it is best for my feet not to always exercise in the same pair. I think I wore the Pumas last time, so I should wear the New Balances. I should make it to the gym by 10:00, which will give me two hours to get my routine in before the noon-time rush. I just purchased a new pair of lifting gloves I need to remember to put in my gym bag before I leave the condo.

I will come home and shower after the gym and make myself a smoothie, because I will be starving, and I do not want to be so famished that I rush over to the Curry House and gulp down all my food. Also, if I am too hungry, I will be more likely to change my mind and duck into another restaurant on my way to Little Tokyo. I will stroll around a little before lunch and buy some green tea and a teapot. A store selling Japanese housewares on the ground floor of the mall was recommended to me for its ceramics, and I can go next door to the supermarket for tea. I want to stop drinking coffee when I get home from work and substitute green tea in order to consume less caffeine.

After lunch I will return home and take a nap, and I will make myself tea in the new pot when I wake up. I will then decide how to spend the evening.

I return my mug and plate to the employee at the counter and go up to my apartment. Indeed, the track jacket looks super with the tank top and the shorts. Two women smile at me on the way to the gym.

Workouts in the gym become habitual. Not only do you repeat the same lifts with the same weights, you also see the same people most nights. Exercising at an irregular time is like visiting a gym in a new city: all unfamiliar faces.

The most notable unfamiliar face is this adorable guy struggling to do military presses on the bench beside me as I do flies. Even with small weights he is struggling to keep his arms steady during the lift, clenching his face in concentration. Maybe he should be using a machine rather than free weights, but I like having him beside me. His tank top has a thin white band around the edges, and the cloth is gray-blue with just a touch of green, a color that would not look out of place as the finish on a classic Jaguar. He is concentrating so intently that I'm certain he doesn't notice me looking at him in the mirror as I rest between sets, slouched over, with my elbows on my knees. I do a final set, return my weights to the rack, and walk to the water fountain.

I'm certain I saw him checking me out earlier, so it would not be inappropriate to start a conversation. I do not want a phone number or a lunch date or random midweek-afternoon sex. A quick flirtation is all I want. Just a smile from him or a clever remark showing he noticed me, too, and he feels as playful and invigorated as I do on this day.

After working through all the lifts in my chest-and-triceps routine, I grab a fresh towel, change the program on my iPod, and run for half an hour on the treadmill. I sit in the Jacuzzi for a while afterwards, since the heat on my tired muscles helps take away any soreness I might feel the next day.

I shower off quickly after the Jacuzzi; I will take a real shower at home. My cute guy is walking into the shower as I walk out and gives me a broad smile. I feel great as I walk to my locker to finish drying off and dress. I've gotten exactly what I wanted.

When I get to Little Tokyo I easily find the store with the housewares. It is full of Japanese plates, cups, bowls, and tea sets. After seeing this blue-gray glazed pot the same color as the flirty boy's tank top, I'm sure I've found the pot I want. The handle is wrapped in some bamboo-like cord, and there is a second glaze, a deep brown, that is worked into the top of the pot and drips down into the blue. My cell phone starts vibrating as I look at the matching cups, trying to decide between the small, Japanese-style cups and the larger, American-style mugs with handles. It is Russ on the phone.

"Look, I'm sorry to bug you at work," he says after we exchange greetings.

I tell him that I have the day off and that I am buying a teapot in Little Tokyo.

"I really like the ones with the little mesh baskets inside for the tea leaves. Tea aficionados will tell you they don't make such good tea because the leaves cannot diffuse around so easily—but they are so much easier to clean, and I can't tell the difference in taste. Wait; is this for you or a gift?"

"The pot is for me," I answer. "I'm trying to cut down on coffee. I'm buying some green tea and a pot to brew it in. I'm hoping loose-leaf tea will taste a lot better than the stuff in tea bags."

"So here's why I am calling. There is a special screening tonight—one night only—of Krzysztov Kieslowski's *Red*. If you're not busy, I wanted to see if you want to go. Sorry about the short notice. I know you're a planner, Damon. Have you seen it?"

"Yeah. I own the DVD."

"Great! But a film like that, it is always the best on the big screen."

"Well, I'd love to see the movie tonight."

"Really? You don't need to clear it with your Palm Pilot first?"

"What time?"

"The movie is at 8:00. I'd suggest dinner, but I'm stuck in class until 6:00, so it would be too rushed. I'll grab a quick sandwich after lecture and come to your place. The movie's at the ArcLight so it won't take too long to get there. I'll go online and get us tickets ahead of time. Look, I've got this tea you should totally try. It is amazing. We can break in your new pot before we head to the theater."

"Cool, I'll see you sometime between six and seven."

"All right, Damon, see you then."

Russ is an aberration. Our relationship makes no sense. He is in his final undergraduate year at USC and should be nothing more than another young buck I fucked once and never saw again. We met at Seth and Lucinda's annual summer pool party. To save money, the City of Lomita moved its Independence Day fireworks to the preceding weekend when the rates are lower. Rather than celebrating the birth of our nation, the fireworks now commemorate Lomita's secession from Torrance and subsequent incorporation. The celebration is called Founder's Day in memory of the brave Lomitians who helped incorporate the two-square-mile town. Lucinda and Seth live a couple blocks away from the park where the fireworks are launched and have a great view of the display from their front yard. They always throw a big party to coincide with the fireworks.

Russ was at the party since he was working a summer internship at Lucinda's firm. The party was one of those languid affairs that begins in the late afternoon with appetizers and swims in the pool and stretches into the early morning, everyone lounging or dancing, all candles and white-wine sangria. An afternoon of subtle flirtation between Russ and me gave way to hours of talk under the arbor strung with paper lanterns—which gave way to the two of us making out in Seth and Lucinda's Jacuzzi.

We went back to my place after the party. That was the only night we ever spent together; we haven't as much as kissed since then. What did happen is that we started bumping into each other all the time. We liked the same restaurants, the same cafés, the same music, the same clubs, the same movies. So we became friends, which is especially comforting since Travis is away so much now.

As friendly and open as he is, there is an anachronistic formality about Russ. I've never seen him wear tennis shoes; he's loath to call people by their first names. In another, this might be misconstrued as preppy stuffiness, a sort of presumption, but with Russ it is all earnestness and guilelessness. I have the feeling sometimes that he just walked out of a Wes Anderson film. He's certainly no prude and has a mischievous side he only shows when he is really comfortable with someone.

THE CURRY HOUSE IS UNASSUMING: decorated in pale woods and located in the second floor of a shopping plaza that is largely vacated. The accretion of memories alone can explain its heightened significance.

I am seated at a small table, and I place the bag with the teapot on the chair opposite me. I scan the menu but choose the special: crab and shrimp cakes with a spicy curry.

They serve the salad so rapidly I need not consider how to occupy myself alone at the table. Then the entrée arrives: a large plateau of rice topped with three of the cakes, shredded nori on top of that, and circled by a moat of the curry sauce. The sauce is pleasantly spicy, and the cakes are very lightly battered and fried without being greasy. Ordering something I hadn't eaten before, I decide in hindsight, was a wise decision.

The trio of pickles that come with the meals is what I have missed the most about the restaurant. A slightly sweet red radish is my favorite, and somehow the pickles are even more special due to the small metal tongs that hang from the side of the condiment container, tongs one uses to place the pickle on one's plate. But I am a fan of the briny green cucumber, too. The pickles are arranged in their own tricolor: green, white, red. I am happy Russ called about the movie tonight.

My only disappointment is that the crab cakes had more sauce than most of the dishes. Usually, there is plenty of extra rice to eat with the pickle. It is all right, though: I am now free anytime to return and order something with more rice. A bit of a walk home, and I am ready for my nap.

I turn off the ringers on my cell phone and my landline, undress, and bury myself beneath a quilt on the couch. It feels less like a nap than a descent to the bottom of a deep well: dark, balsamic.

The buzzer I awake to is my doorbell. It is dark, and I am disoriented. I am wearing nothing, so I bundle myself in the quilt and stumble to the door, knocking my knee on the coffee table and flipping on the lights as I unlatch the lock and open the door to a bemused Russ.

"I'm guessing you were asleep," he says.

"Sorry, I didn't realize I was so tired. It was light out when I fell asleep. I thought I'd wake up long before you got here."

"Relax. I didn't have to buzz you from downstairs because a neighbor let me in. The buzzing would have given you at least a little warning."

"We're not supposed to let people in like that."

"I agreed to stop by his place and suck him off after we get back from the flick," he says in a deadpan manner, although it is obvious he is being facetious.

"He was cute, at least?"

"Hideous. Are you going to let me in?"

"No, I'm laughing to myself about what the eavesdropping old lady across the hall must think of you after this conversation."

"Good lord, I'm sure this doesn't fluster her in the least after all the things she's seen you drag in. Seriously, if you let me in, I'll make a pot of tea as you change out of your blanket." He pulls out a plastic baggie filled with the tea from his pocket and shakes it in front of me. "It's really good."

"OK, get in here."

"Where's the tea pot."

"On the drying rack. I washed it when I got home."

I go into my bedroom to change and hear him clanging pots to look for a kettle in which to boil water.

"You didn't listen to me. This doesn't have the wire thingy," he yells.

"I liked the color," I respond as I pull on my pants.

I go into the bathroom to fix my hair and brush my teeth. I can hear Russ still talking to me but can't make out the words. By the time I'm all dressed he is pouring hot water into the pot.

"Smell this, Damon," he lifts the teapot's lid, inhales some steam, and moves aside for me to do the same. I incline over the pot and breathe deeply. It smells like a damp cellar.

"Russ, what is that? It's moldy!"

"Trust me. It is called Purah-The. It has been aged underground for a decade. Just let it steep a few more minutes. Say, why did you take the day off?"

"I turned in a big grant proposal yesterday."

"Is there still money in Brownian motors?"

"I won't know for a little while, but I'm happy with what I submitted."

"You really do have *Red* on DVD. I looked while you were de-blanketing. What's your favorite scene?"

"The end, I think, when she emerges from the crash and is— finally—in the arms of the young judge. Whenever I feel confused or anxious—which I suppose is much more often than I like to let on to people—I always feel like I just want to fall into some…well, lowest-energy state…just emerge from the wreckage into that place I'm always trying to get to."

"Lowest-energy state?"

"A ground state, completely relaxed."

"OK, the tea is ready," says Russ. He pours two cupfuls, using a small sieve to catch the leaves, which he puts back into the pot. "You can use the leaves several times. Maybe you'll want another cup when you get home from the movie. And this tea is so special; you won't want to waste it."

He carries the cups to the coffee table and sits in an armchair. I sit on the couch. I take a sip of the tea. It is of the earth; somehow musty and mineral-infused without being muddy—smooth and polished. It tastes of age, of geologic time, of flowing mountains. It suggests profound depths.

"I am always skeptical about such things," says Russ, "but it is said to be the most healing of the teas. I just like it for the taste."

"So what is your favorite scene in the movie?"

"Probably when she helps the old hunched lady with the recycling. After seeing two protagonists sit passively in the earlier films, there is such triumph in that small gesture when she finally rises from the bench. And something about the clink of her heels on the pavement as she walks away. It is like her ability to finally connect is linked with her dignity."

"Are you still seeing tank-top guy?"

"Seriously, Damon, I never once have seen him in sleeves! How can someone do that? I mean, there were muscle shirts, so it wasn't all tank tops. And once when it was really cold he wore a fleece vest. So at least there was a little variety. I think we broke up last night."

"What happened?"

"He couldn't believe I wanted to see this movie rather than go to eighteen-and-over night at some club in WeHo."

"Fuck sleeveless guy."

"Exactly, fuck him. Fuck him and his curious inability to cover his arms." Russ laughs deeply, leans back in the armchair, and crosses his legs, balancing his cup on his knee. I'm sure he secretly wants to smoke cigars and own a basset hound.

"And you," he asks, "nothing outside the usual shenanigans?"

"Nothing of consequence."

"To two bachelors." He raises his tea in a toast to us. "Chinese tea, European cinema. What more do we need?" He takes a drink. "So I've got something to run by you, since I know you are such a big Pavement fan."

My eyes must bulge out of my head just hearing the band name. "Back in the '90s they were like the only band that existed for me," I say.

"I know. That's why I need to talk to you. I've been going back and downloading all their old work. *Crooked Rain, Crooked Rain* was the only CD I owned. I never noticed this at the time, but do you think there is an undercurrent of gayness in Pavement lyrics?"

"Totally," I say. "The liner notes for *Wowee Zowee* begin with 'dick sucking fool at pussy licking school.' I always figured he was bi."

"That clinches my theory," says Russ. "You miss out on those things with the digital versions. I started thinking about it because of that line in 'Stop Breathing': 'Nothing gets me off so completely / as when you put it down / ten feet down in the ground.' I figured that line, and all the mining references in the early singles, are about anal sex."

"I had this bootleg recording of a live show," I say, "that had an early version of 'Blackout.' The chorus of this early, live version is Stephen screaming 'Big gay heart, big gay heart,' and all the lyrics seem to be about being young and gay: 'You've got no one when you're talking...no one has a clue.' And 'Blackout' seems an apt title, the way gayness seems erased from everything around you when you're in high school. You learn Shakespeare's 'Let me not to the marriage of true minds—' sonnet in English class, but the very central fact that it is written from one guy to another is left out. The way the local library subscribes to every obscure magazine available but manages to skip *The Advocate*. At the time, the song seemed written for me. I was so upset when the album was released and the 'big gay heart' lyrics were changed. I've never known another Pavement fan I could talk to about this."

"You have to give me that track," says Russ. "And how about, 'Increase had them outed and they burned on open fires'?"

"From 'Give it a Day'? I think he is saying 'mounted' rather than 'outed.'"

We figure we should leave for the movie. I put the cups in the kitchen and grab a jacket. We continue talking about Pavement during our drive to the ArcLight. I tell Russ about this Pavement DVD I just bought that has all their old videos and interviews with the band. Besides the CD of bootlegged performances, I agree to let him borrow the DVD as well.

4

Denise's prediction that she and Travis would break up is soon realized. They stopped seeing each other a few days before the planned dinner with the Hungarian string quartet. This leaves Seth, Lucinda, and me to dine with the visiting musicians. Only two members of the string quartet are Hungarians: the cellist, who turns out to be the one Travis has been corresponding with by email, and the first violinist. The cellist is a charming woman with a Hungarian name none of us can pronounce. She speaks fluent, if accented, English. Unlike the cellist, the first violinist's English is nearly incomprehensible. Undaunted, he speaks with joyous abandon and refuses to allow the others to act as translators no matter how baffled we become at the jumble of words that spill out of him in his singsong accent. The second violinist is a German woman with a perfect British enunciation.

Seth and Lucinda are taking their coats and asking if they

want drinks, when the viola player walks in a little behind the rest. He is the Greek statue we saw at the Getty: the same large eyes and the same relaxed mouth. He is dressed completely in conservative black, but slacks and a buttoned shirt can not hide his full chest and thighs. Even placid Travis reflexively gulps in an extra breath of air at the site of the man.

The statue's name is Nathan. He is American. He moved to London after high school to study music. After finishing his time at the conservatory, he moved to Budapest and joined the quartet.

"So you are Travis," Nathan says as he shakes his hand after shaking mine. "It is incredibly kind of you to have a bunch of strangers in your home like this. Your cousin said you are a softie, but this still feels like an imposition."

Travis introduces me and explains that he could not have hosted the quartet without the help of Lucinda, Seth, and me.

"I'm really confused," says Travis. "I didn't realize you knew my cousin. I thought the connection with my cousin was through the cellist."

"No, I can see why you assumed that through the emails. Sara was handling all the arrangements for here in LA because I had split away from the group for a few weeks to visit my family in Portland. I lost my laptop in New York. My folks haven't yet entered the computer age, so it was just easier for her to make all the contacts. You don't remember me, then? We met a long time ago."

Travis admits that he can't recall meeting Nathan before.

"I was in high school at the time, dating your cousin," says

Nathan. "We took this crazy road trip to Southern California during spring break of our senior year. We stopped one night out where you were living—out near Riverside somewhere."

"It was in a trailer park?" asks Travis.

"Yes, it was. You were just a kid. When we got there, you were crying because of a broken toy—some robot, I think."

"My transformer. I remember. You and my cousin took me out for ice cream." Travis smiles broadly.

"We took you out to cheer you up," says Nathan, also breaking into a broad grin.

"To the Dairy Queen."

"So, yes, way back then, that was me." Nathan touches Travis on the forearm lightly as he says this.

"You were dating my cousin. I can't believe it."

"Obviously your family didn't know. We broke up when I moved to London but always stayed in touch. He even lived with my parents for a time when things got really bad at his home. This is so strange: I was still picturing you as a little kid in corduroy shorts when we were coming over here."

"And you're only here in LA a short time?"

"Until April, so it is a good stay. I wish it was summer, though. I so miss the ocean; I was hoping to spend as much time at the beach as possible. Maybe go to Venice Beach."

"No, that's all tourists, you don't want to go there," says Travis. I'm quite sure that Travis hasn't been to the beach in years and doesn't know anything about which beaches to go to.

"Where do you suggest?" asks Nathan.

"Damon knows the perfect beach in Santa Barbara. It is impossible to find, so only locals go there."

"That sounds wonderful," says Nathan.

"Cliffs above you, not crowded at all. It is in town but you feel like you are in a secluded cove up the coast. And part of it is clothing optional." I have never taken Travis to the nude beach he is talking about; his description is second hand from me.

"What is it called?" asks Nathan.

I say, "More Mesa Beach," and Travis simultaneously says, "The Meditation Beach." Travis giggles and says, "More Meditation Mesa Beach," and somehow thinks Nathan is going to believe this. "Meditation Beach" is a euphemism for "nude beach" that my boyfriend and I used to use.

"I guess I can hope for an Indian summer," says Nathan. He even picks up a little of Travis's giggle.

"It might be warm enough in April," I say. "It isn't manicured like city beaches. There's seaweed and driftwood and anything else that washed ashore. It is all part of it."

Lucinda walks over and introduces herself. "I'm afraid the boys have lost their manners," she says. "Travis, why not let your friend sit down and see if he wants a drink."

I go back to the kitchen to get appetizers. Lucinda has taken care to make sure everyone has drinks. Since Travis doesn't often drink alcohol and Seth is a recovering alcoholic, we have plenty of juice and soda water and iced tea. The quartet, Lucinda, and I drink wine.

At first, I was uncomfortable drinking in front of Seth even though he has been sober for the better part of a decade. He explained to me that he went through such hell at his bottom and worked diligently enough at the steps since then that alcohol now posed no temptation for him. Since meeting Seth, my main strategy for dealing with recovering alcoholics at social events I'm hosting is to buy expensive bottled water and serve it in my best glasses. Twists of lime are recommended. Being part of the ritual of drinking with the group is still maintained, even if the substance in the glass is fundamentally different.

While he avoids wine-based sauces, Seth is amazing in the kitchen. I've convinced a lot of people that I'm a good cook. The truth is that I'm simply good at following recipes; it reminds me a lot of running experiments when I was a graduate student. Seth is something else, a natural cook, the kind of man who can re-create at home the food he tastes in a restaurant. The two of us spent the afternoon making dinner. Travis wanted everything vegetarian since it is his kitchen. I came prepared with photocopied recipes for caramelized-onion pizza, butternut squash tart, mushroom and asparagus lasagna, and all the ingredients I would need. Seth came with bags of herbs from his garden, winter produce from the farmer's market, olives, cheeses, and no apparent plan. His part of the meal lavishly eclipses mine.

We pictured a foursome of stern, mirthless Central Europeans, but the party is jovial and boisterous. Even with the furniture we've purchased, the loft is largely empty space, so Lucinda brought dozens of candles in various jewel-toned votives and scattered them on every accessible surface. One feels like one has drifted into a Kandinsky.

It is long after dinner when our food settles enough for dessert. I am in the kitchen getting dessert together when the cellist comes up to talk.

"Is Travis your boyfriend?" she asks.

I must have looked a little surprised, because the cellist apologizes.

"Nathan warned me no to be so blunt with Americans," she says.

I tell her that there is no reason to apologize and that Travis is just an old friend.

"Good. Then any flirting between him and Nathan, it's not a problem."

"Not at all," I say.

"I've been around the world with that guy, and he can find an attractive man anywhere to hit on. It is a thing above what most men can do." Sara puts slices of the spice cake I am cutting on dessert plates while we talk.

She tells me she is still having problems expressing complex or abstract ideas in English. Because she needs to communicate a lot when the quartet is in residence, she has been watching a lot of American TV and reading American magazines to help improve her English. Eventually, our conversation leads to her telling me about this particular *New Yorker* article that made her angry.

"This article was about some language spoken in Alaska," she says, "some tribal tongue. The last native speaker just died, and the author was recalling a visit with the dead woman a few months previously."

"That doesn't seem like anything to get angry about," I say.

"A statement the author makes is what made me angry. This Alaska language—I can not recall its name—split off from its nearest neighboring language about three thousand years ago. This closest relative language was also some arctic people's language. The author went on and on about how incredible for a language to be distinct for so long and how it can only be explained by isolation in this far northern bay."

"Again, why did this upset you?"

"The author must not know languages well. Hungarian split off from its closest relative three thousand years ago and has had no contact with a similar language since then."

"Isn't it related to Russian?"

"What? Not at all!" says the cellist. "Your English is closer to Russian than Hungarian is. The closest relatives of Hungarian are, well, some tribal languages spoken in Siberia. Again the arctic people. Finnish is the closest relative in Europe. But there is not a common vocabulary, only a similarity in grammar."

"And you were mad because the author should have mentioned that Hungarian, too, survived for so long?"

"Well, unlike the Alaska language, Hungarian still lives. That is part of it. But I think it is amazing because Hungarian did not do this tucked away in a fjord nobody knew about for twenty-nine hundred of its three thousand years. It did it right in the dead center of Europe. It did it surrounded by Germans and Romanians and Slavs all over the place: Southern Slavs, Western Slavs, Eastern Slavs. How incredible for a language to survive like that: being lorded over by Turks, then Austrians, then Russians, and still keeping its identity. Have you been to Hungary?"

"No, the closest I've gotten is Vienna. I'm going back next June for a conference," I say.

"Really? You must go to Budapest."

"I haven't planned anything yet. I should have time."

"It is too bad; the quartet will be in Japan. But we will tell you where to go."

The cellist and I take the slices of cake to everybody. Seth and the two violinists talk at the table while the rest of us sit around the coffee table. I brewed some coffee, but everyone wants more wine. I bring Travis some tea.

"Why don't you drink alcohol?" the cellist asks Travis. She looks at me, shrugs her shoulders, and jokes about the hopelessness of her trying not to be so direct in her questions.

"I really don't enjoy alcohol. It isn't a religious thing," says Travis.

"Really? Is this true?" asks the cellist.

"Travis drank a little when we were in college but never really perfected the technique like some of us," says Lucinda. Back then she could drink more than anybody I knew; she still might be able to. I can never tell when Lucinda is drunk.

"The last time I saw Travis drink," I say, "was my first year of graduate school. It was at a Halloween party; he had come up to visit me in Santa Barbara."

Travis interrupts me, "We really don't need to tell this story."

Nathan puts his hand on Travis's knee. They are sitting next to each other on the couch. Nathan says, "I think this story sounds really interesting."

Travis tries to just give the short form of the story: "It was Halloween in Santa Barbara when Damon was a graduate student there, and I had too much to drink."

Lucinda sits on the couch on the opposite side of Travis from Nathan. She has to lean forward to speak directly to Nathan. She alternates this leaning forward with half-turning her torso in the opposite direction to keep the cellist in the conversation. She is not going to let Travis off the hook and will help me in telling the whole embarrassing tale: "You have to understand that the area around the university where all the students live is one of the most infamous party towns on the West Coast; it is called Isla Vista. On any weekend the streets are flooded with kids walking to parties; the smell of spilled beer is everywhere; and for some reason old couches are dragged into the street and set on fire. Halloween used to be the most insane party weekend of the year. Kids traveled there from all over California to spend the holiday."

I pick up the story from Lucinda: "By the time I was there for graduate school, the police were really trying to crack down on the Halloween parties. They blockaded the central streets. They especially targeted underage drinking. We were twenty-three or twenty-four at the time, so it should not have been an issue. The Halloween Travis came for a visit we went to a party at another engineering graduate student's apartment, and Travis started doing shots. Remember, this is someone who usually won't even have a beer, and he is doing shots with this girl who starts talking to him about poetry. Wasn't she dressed up like Pocahontas?"

"She was the only one at the party I could talk to," says Travis. "I don't even know how she ended up there. Everyone else was an engineer or a scientist. Everyone else responded to questions with one-word answers, when I tried to make conversation and exhibited borderline autistic behavior."

"Our Damon is high functioning for an engineer," says Lucinda.

"And my pretty friend was dressed as Sacagawea, not Pocahontas," says Travis. "She was a Whitman scholar. She was reciting 'Out of the Cradle Endlessly Rocking' to me as we were drinking. We would discuss every line, savor it."

"All of a sudden I look over, and Travis was not there," I say.

"Sacagawea and I decided we had to go to the beach," says Travis. Since Nathan is listening so intently and laughing along as we tell the story, Travis seems not to mind telling some of the details himself. "We wanted to say the lines where we could hear the surf. *Out of the ninth month midnight*...I was very, very drunk. Anyway, we were cutting across a park to get to the beach, and there was a woman dressed as a gypsy, with a basket on her arm, just twirling and dancing alone in the park, with scarves trailing her movement. When we walked by, she started dancing around us. She reached into her basket, which was filled with condoms, and handed one to each of us. I put mine in my pocket, thanked her, and she spun away. Sacagawea and I kept walking towards the ocean."

"Meanwhile I left the party and returned to my apartment, because it was so late. I figured Travis would show up eventually," I say. "I called my boyfriend—we were fighting because he hadn't driven up for the holiday. I wanted to stay off the phone in case Travis called, so we didn't talk long. I fell asleep on the couch, still waiting to hear from him. It was 8:00 the next morning when the phone finally rang. Travis was calling from the police station in downtown Santa Barbara. He had spent the night in the drunk tank and had just been released."

"We had bumped into a few police officers after leaving the park," says Travis. "They had asked for IDs to make sure we were over twenty-one. I pulled my driver's license out of my back pocket and gave it to the officer. He just kept staring at my license in his hand and asking me if this was some sort of joke, over and over, each time more accusingly. I couldn't figure out what he was so upset about."

The cellist pours more wine into my glass, and I thank her. Lucinda continues the story, "It turns out what Travis thought was his driver's license was really the condom the gypsy had given him. He handed the police officer a condom from his back pocket and the officer took Travis for some sort of jackass. They hauled him to the drunk tank for the night."

"It was humiliating," says Travis. "The drunk tank is a cement cube with one toilet, open to the sky, a drain in the middle, and about a dozen drunk guys. I threw up on myself in the middle of the night and had no way of cleaning it up."

"He was a mess by the time I got to him," I say. "I haven't seen him drink since."

Everyone is laughing. "All because of a girl," says the cellist. "She must have been beautiful."

Travis thinks for a moment before he answers, "It wasn't her; it was the poetry. The words were like freedom. The poetry intoxicated me as much as the tequila, as much as the girl. It was like I wanted to feel the sand at the beach, just sit there on the beach at night, more than anything."

"C'mon, Travis," says Nathan. "It had to be infatuation to drive you to such things."

"No, that would be Damon in college." Travis glares at me. He clearly wants to get back at me for telling the story about his arrest by telling an embarrassing story about me. "Our freshman year, we lived in the same dorm. That's how we met. We were about eighteen, and Damon falls madly in love with this guy down the hall. What is most important to remember about this story, however, is that Damon was totally sober the whole time. He doesn't need alcohol to make a fool out of himself."

"In my defense," I say, "the guy was unbelievably hot. He was

68

Brazilian..."

"Enough said," interrupts the cellist. "They're hot and crazy."

"He went on to do some modeling," I say.

"Honey," says Lucinda, "having naked photos of you posted on the Internet does not make you a model. The ironic part of all this is that the Brazilian messed around with half the dorm by the end of the year, but Damon decides he is in love and doesn't get to so much as make out with the Brazilian."

"I was young, and he was terribly charismatic," I say as an explanation. "That Brazilian guy, he could smile at you and make you think you two shared a private joke of which the rest of the planet was ignorant. He could tell stories like nobody else. A trip to the store to buy toilet paper could be riveting, the way he told it."

"Anyway," says Lucinda, "it all started one night in the cafeteria. We were eating together and joking around. We were making up this scenario where we were superheroes in disguise. It was silly, like we were part of a comic book set in an undergraduate dorm."

"I was Cereal Man," I say, "able to shoot high fiber out my fingertip and trap bad guys in crunchy goodness. I hated the cafeteria food and ate cereal for three meals a day. It was a running joke."

Lucinda says, "And Brazilian guy, I think he was just Super Brazilian Guy. We weren't too creative with that one."

I say, "The joke kept escalating until we went back to our dorm rooms and started dressing like superheroes. Super Brazilian

Guy wore some long underwear as tights; I wore boxers with stars and skyrockets pulled on over sweatpants. He wore a cycling jersey; I had a bath towel safety-pinned around my shoulders as a cape. We both had masks, of course."

"I think Cereal Man's mask was actually a pair of swim goggles," says Lucinda, "Super Brazilian Guy, inexplicably, also wore a green lamé bow tie. Since the two guys were so full of themselves and their secret powers, I dared them to sneak across campus in full super-regalia and steal a box of cornflakes from the campus convenience store."

"And Super Brazilian Guy and Cereal Man did it!" I say. "We jumped in and out of hedges to stay out of the view of bicyclists, snuck behind walls, concealed ourselves behind trees. We snuck into the convenience store while the cashier was distracted by a pack of binging sorority girls. It felt like we did have superpowers. I felt like we could fly. We got back to the dorm with the cornflakes and were close to getting back upstairs and presenting our booty to the group's mastermind, Lucinda…"

"…until they got into the landing one flight away from my room—secret lair I think we were calling it that night—and heard someone opening the door from the hallway into the landing," says Lucinda. We have told this story together so many times that we can complete one another's sentences. "Maybe they could have run upstairs as fast as possible and avoid being seen, but they decided to squeeze against the wall and hide behind the opening door."

I return to the story: "What Lucinda hasn't told you, and

you really need to know this to appreciate the next part, is that my roommates that year were three football players from the Central Valley. Nice guys, but total jocks. We were civil, but never really buddies. They had photos of pheasants they had shot during hunting on the walls and invited me home to see the rice harvest. And all three were gigantic."

"So you have to imagine our outlandishly dressed gay boys hiding behind the opening door, somehow thinking they won't be seen, praying the burly football player Hank will lumber by obliviously, the two of them holding their breaths lest they make the slightest sound," says Lucinda.

"And of course Hank feels the door push against Super Brazilian Guy and myself. We would have had to be an inch think for that plan to work."

"What does the football player do?" asks Nathan.

"Hank just stands there, looks me straight in the eye for what feels like ten minutes, showing no expression on his face. We are both frozen like that; he had to look down at me since he was so much taller. And then he just starts laughing. He walks downstairs, still laughing, and never mentions it to me the whole rest of the year we lived together. And it totally ruined the vibe between me and Brazilian guy. Had we made it back to Lucinda's room, we would have been so hyped, I know we would have gone back to Brazilian guy's room, and he would have been the first boy I ever kissed. He was so embarrassed by the incident that he totally avoided me after that."

"And you, Lucinda?" asks the cellist. "You must have been as bad as the boys."

"You bet, but I was also a lot more discreet than these fools."

This goes on late into the night. We clean up a little but mostly decide to leave everything for the morning. Seth and Lucinda don't want to drive home, so they decide to spend the night in my spare bedroom. The cellist and the violinists walk outside with us, but Nathan stays behind. We make sure the musicians get into a taxi before we leave.

Before joining Seth in the spare bedroom, Lucinda talks to me in the kitchen while we drink some water.

"Can you believe Travis?" says Lucinda. "Have you ever seen him act so giddy? Where did that come from?"

"I can't believe Nathan is spending the night there," I say.

"And Travis seemed totally cool with that."

"He was beaming."

"Well, I guess it is a good thing for Travis," she says.

"Definitely a good thing."

"It has to be a good thing, right? For him to be excited like that?"

"Most definitely a good thing, or at least not a bad thing."

"Yes, at least not a bad thing."

5

IN THE DAYS BEFORE TIGHTENED AIRPORT SECURITY, Travis would go to LAX and read in the terminals. He would watch the crowds departing and arriving, the tearful good-byes and the tender reunions, daydream about the cities on the schedule board, and buy snacks at the newsstands like a real traveler. Now he hangs out at Union Station. When he grows restless in the station, he takes excursions on the metro to distant parts of the city and back. The Gold Line is his favorite, he says, because it is all above ground and because the trip to Pasadena is so leisurely: taking half an hour to cover the distance any other commuter train could traverse in ten minutes. On this drizzly afternoon a man a few rows ahead of Travis is singing what sounds like a torch song in French. Nobody mocks the singer or interrupts. Travis puts down his book and leans his forehead against the train's window, watching the Arroyo Grande pass by.

I pick him up at Union Station so we can head to West Hollywood for Allan's birthday party. Travis told me to call his cell phone when I arrive so he can meet me at the curb, but I am intentionally a half hour early so I can park my car and walk around the station. Union Station occurred at some perfect moment when Spanish Revival architecture collided with the Arts and Crafts movement. There is no better building in the city. I find Travis in the main hall, seated sideways on one of the wood benches, with his book propped against his bent legs. I sit in the bank of seats opposite him and say nothing.

I picked the color scheme in my apartment to match the tiles on the wall here. I am staring upward at the wood beams in the ceiling when Travis asks me if I am ready to leave. I'm not sure how long he knew I was there before talking to me. We go to my car.

We are most of the way to Allan's before I ask about Nathan. Travis and I have talked multiple times since last weekend's dinner party, but never about this. All he says is that they have been hanging out a lot, and that Nathan would have gone to the party today but has practice with the quartet, and that he might meet up with us later if he can get a lift to West Hollywood.

"So are you hanging out as in buddies or hanging out as in something romantic?" I ask.

"Something romantic, I guess."

"You've messed around with him?"

"We're taking it slow. You know, Damon, we wouldn't be having this conversation if Nathan were a girl."

74

"You haven't gone out with a guy for years; it is out of the ordinary for you. Of course I am going to ask about it."

"Man, woman—what does it matter? I'd like to think whomever I date is independent of their physical nature. Gender, age, race—it is all fleeting."

Allan lives in one of those neighborhoods where only residents with permits can park on the streets. His driveway is already full, so I park blocks away on Crescent Heights. The sky has cleared, but the sun is already setting. Travis is annoyed with me. He says he wants to call Nathan, since he is supposed to be on his dinner break at this time. He says he'll meet me at the house and starts walking in the opposite direction with his phone at his ear. I heft Allan's gift out of the trunk and walk back to the house with the package perched on my shoulder.

I walk up the drive and find Allan in the back lighting coals in the barbecue. He says he's relieved the rain has stopped because he had his heart set on grilling tonight. He also says he has dry wood piled in the garage and will start a bonfire later in the fire pit he and Ron just finished making. Allan is not a tall man and was probably painfully slight in high school. He goes to the gym as much as I do and has one of those physiques that isn't bulky but tightly knotted without a bit of body fat. He's wearing a tank top and baseball cap. It is cold and getting colder. He scrapes the grill clean and talks about the projects he and Ron are working on around the house, but I am preoccupied by the urge to take off my coat and wrap it around his shoulders. I lean the present against the house in a place where the pavement is dry.

Allan is an accountant. He works at one of the large firms downtown and bought this house early in the year. It is a small two-bedroom; the previous owners were elderly and let it fall into disrepair. Allan is fixing it up largely himself, with the help of Ron and also Travis when he is in town.

CJ comes out the back door with two open beer bottles and hands one to each of us. CJ is a boy today. He kisses me on the cheek.

"You said there were dry chairs in the garage?" asks CJ. Allan nods in assent, and CJ goes to fetch three of them.

"I figure us men can sit out here and tend the fire," says CJ. "Where's Travis?"

"He's on his cell phone," I say. "He'll be here in a minute. Maybe I should put the present inside. I'll be right back."

"Honey," says CJ, "let me do it. You just got here." He takes the gift and goes inside before I can protest.

Allan and I talk about plumbing.

"I just can't wait to get everything done. It so bothers me not to have everything in its right place," he says. "All I can feel is the anticipation of completeness."

I ask Allan if he purchased a new hot-water heater yet. He tells me about the resistive heater he is considering: it is more efficient than conventional gas heaters and so small it can fit under the house.

CJ comes back, "I leave you two alone for just a moment and

come back to a bunch of techie shit. The discussion about bathroom tile earlier was much more lively." Johnny comes out with some odd-colored cocktail he has mixed. He gives me a hug and gets a chair for himself.

In the kitchen window I see a very tall and very pale man with a shaved head, wearing a woven Peruvian folk vest, no shirt, and some sort of curving Maori pendant. As quickly as he popped into the window, he is gone. A moment later Lucinda is in the window, washing a glass at the sink, turning her head to talk to someone standing outside my view.

"Did you guys see a really tall, bald hippie guy?" I ask.

"Some friend of Ron's," says Allan. "He's even older than he looks."

"Actually, I was just talking to him and found him very interesting," says CJ.

"How so?" asks Allan.

"His opinions," says CJ, "about stuff."

Johnny reaches over, takes CJ's hand and kisses it. He leans back in the lawn chair and plays with his boyfriend's hair while we talk. He is a rangy, uncoordinated bloke, sexy in a way that is interesting and entirely unconventional. The pertinent question, in terms of Johnny, is what do you do with your life if you are a trust-fund baby, if concern over financial security completely factors out of the equation?

He was born with a craving for transcendence without possessing a sense of the spiritual—that volatile combination that organized religion has tried to extinguish on a societal level. His chosen outlets have been sex and drug use, mainly drug use. An acquaintance (one of the few he had at the time) chided him into volunteering at the Gay and Lesbian Resource Center five years ago, and since then he has become a volunteer-work junkie. It has given him a social net he always lacked before, a reason to leave his house, and increased responsibility. He still insists illicit drugs can be consumed safely in moderation, and one of his five volunteer positions is campaigning for marijuana legalization, but his use has scaled back enormously since the charity addiction kicked in. He fixes bicycles on Saturday mornings for a gay youth cycling group in Santa Monica; he had never touched a wrench before starting his work there.

Allan met Johnny soon after Allan tested HIV positive through the fundraising Johnny was doing for AIDS prevention. They were fast friends but never dated. When Johnny met our CJ, however, the two brought out hidden parts of one another. CJ's wanderlust drew Johnny even further out of the insular world he had built for himself in SoCal. They are adventurous travelers, and the extent to which Johnny is a blank slate allows his easy integration into other lands. CJ had based his life around needing nothing from anybody. He is of the world: objects, food, surfaces. Having someone to love has given him a tenderness he previously lacked.

"Damon, you won't believe what I saw flipping through channels the other night," says Allan, "I couldn't sleep, was just tossing in bed and disturbing Ron, so I got up and turned on the TV in the living room. It was really late and I caught just the last thirty seconds of one of the trashy news magazines. I'm not sure what the story was about, but they were showing a clip of these girls—total busty Playboy-type models—frolicking around that Lloyd Wright house where we saw the snake dancing. The two shots I saw were a couple girls in lingerie chasing each other around the central courtyard with the pool and the fire-urn; and the second shot was of three girls bouncing up and down and tickling each other on a couch under those Aztec-style cement sculptures. I recognized the house immediately. I want to know what the story was about. I would have taped it to show you if it had only been on a few more minutes."

A few years ago Johnny had given Allan two tickets for a charity dance performance. There were only about a hundred people attending. The troupe was from San Francisco and performed with snakes. The performance drew on myths centered around serpents and moon cycles and rebirth; it incorporated dance with poetry, chanting, and music from a live ensemble that was mainly percussion and flutes. When the performers weren't holding up snakes—all different types of constrictors—or allowing snakes to reptate around their shoulders, the dancers were twirling flaming staves or descending into and reemerging from the small pool.

The different scenes in the performance didn't really hold together, but Allan was enraptured by the men and women running around in loincloths with leather bands tied around their arms and thighs. Personally, I was enraptured by the building. It was a private residence that I might otherwise never have seen from the inside. Snowden house was modeled after an Aztec temple, and thus gave the performance an authenticity it would have lacked on a conventional stage. This was in the days before Allan and Ron had started dating, so I was lucky he chose to share the ticket with me. Afterwards he said he figured none of our other friends could have handled watching a performance filled with topless women without giggling or freaking out.

Suddenly there is a pounding on the fence behind me. I spill my beer as I jump out of the lawn chair. There is an animal-like wailing. We all stare towards the noise but remain motionless. People are looking out the window and the back door. My adrenalin-shocked heart pounds behind my ribs.

Allan puts down the brush he was using to clean the grill and closes the lid of the barbecue. I decide the noise is definitely a man screaming, but the words are undecipherable.

Allan walks to the fence, and I follow him. I try to stop my hand from quivering. Everyone else hangs back.

"Buddy, you need to calm down," says Allan in a voice that is loud without being aggressive. He keeps walking toward the fence, talking to whoever is behind it. I'm not sure how threatened I should be, but I trust that Allan knows what he is doing and follow him.

"Buddy, this is Allan. You really need to calm down. We are having a party. Remember, I talked to you about it this afternoon. You need to relax. Just go inside and eat some dinner and watch TV."

The screaming and the pounding subside. Allan and I are

standing right at the fence now. I can see a figure on the other side through the slits. He is all shadow. I can't even make out his face. It is certainly just one man causing all the noise.

"I hear voices, Allan, and it makes me nervous," says Buddy.

"It is only my friends," says Allan.

I can hear heavy breathing behind the fence. The shadow then walks away, and I think I can hear a screen door open and slam shut.

"Sorry, everyone," says Allan, "Buddy's a Vietnam vet. He gets angry now and then. It is nothing to worry about. It is just taking him a little time to get used to having us as neighbors. I don't think he does well with change." The fear dissipates. Everyone talks about the guy behind the fence for a while, and then we all return to our drinks and our earlier conversation.

"I'm going inside for a minute," I say.

"Why not stay out here and talk longer?" says CJ. "Tell me more about the Aztec temple. We got interrupted."

"I need to use the bathroom. You are acting really weird tonight, CJ," I say as I go inside.

The kitchen has yet to be touched by Allan: the linoleum is cracking and all the appliances are pea-green. Lucinda, Seth, and Ron are there with a bunch of Allan and Ron's friends. I recognize many of them from previous parties at the house. Ron runs over when I enter and grabs me by the wrist. He pulls me across the room.

"You've got to meet my friend," he says. And I am standing

toe to toe with the bald-headed albino giant. I think all of his clothes are made of hemp. Ron introduces the two of us.

I shake hands with Hemp Guy. Travis comes in the front door, inquires about the birthday boy, and is directed out back.

"That guy looks familiar," says Hemp Guy.

I explain that Travis is a carpenter on *Redecorating Rooms*, and Hemp Guy nods his head in recognition. Lucinda comes over and gives me a big hug. I ask if she and Hemp Guy have already met.

"We were chatting earlier," she says. She asks Hemp Guy if she could steal me away for a minute. "It is one of those best-gal-pal things," she offers as an explanation.

Lucinda and I walk into the front room.

"Best-gal-pal things?" I say when we are out of Hemp Guy's earshot. "Are you about to ask me for a tampon?"

"I need to know what you think of this skirt."

"It looks great, but I've seen you wear it several times before."

"I know. But never with this top."

"Well, you look stunning." I give her a kiss on the cheek. I figure she is feeling insecure about something.

Ron starts yelling for Lucinda from the kitchen. He wants help making margaritas. She rolls her eyes and walks back into the kitchen. Hemp Guy is beside me with a new beer to replace my empty bottle. I ask him how he knows Ron. I still need to use the bathroom.

Hemp Guy tells me how he goes to yoga class with Ron and then starts explaining the type of yoga they practice. He talks about why he started going to class and how it has changed him. He talks about his chakras.

Over the couch Allan has hung one of Ron's paintings, a large canvas with an abstract blocky image of what I think might be a gold Scythian stag. But when I close one eye and tilt my head, I'm inclined to reconsider: I think it is a Weimeramer and a palm tree. Really, I'm just not sure.

Part of the painting looks a little like the inside-out orange camouflage shirt Bill Murray wears during the karaoke scene in *Lost in Translation*. Maybe this could be that scene in the funky glass room where they sing karaoke and Scarlett Johansson wears a pastel wig. I visualize Scarlett Johansson walking around Kyoto. I remember her face as she explores the temple grounds, absorbing the sites around her. I remember her wearing a peacoat and a scarf and hopping across circular stepping stones set in shallow water. I remember monks. These images will replay in my mind until I rent the movie and watch it, to check my recollection and see the gaps in my memory. How intimately our forgetfulness is linked to pleasure. If I could remember the movie perfectly, I'd never want to see it again. If I had total recall I don't think replaying the film in my perfect memory would be as gratifying as being reminded of all the forgotten details and being reminded of the enjoyment those details had brought, that enjoyment also partially forgotten. Was the color of the scarf she was knitting the powder blue of the sweater she wore in the hotel room or the pale rose of the paper cherry-blossom girandole she hung from the ceiling? I think she wore the scarf during the Kyoto trip.

"Wait," I say to Hemp Guy, suddenly roused from my daydream and interrupting something he is explaining about macrobiotic cuisine, "what did you say you did for a living?"

"I work in finance."

"Fucking shit." I realize this is the man Ron said he wanted to set me up with. CJ and Lucinda have been trying to keep me away from him since I got to the party.

"Pardon?"

"Nothing. I'm sorry." I fake a smile. "Pardon me a moment. I just remembered I forgot something in my car." I walk across the kitchen and out the back door. I go out to the sidewalk and finish the bottle of beer. In the most juvenile action I can think of, I huck the bottle down the street. It shatters. I immediately feel guilty when I picture a bicycle getting a flat tire from a glass shard. Lucinda is here.

"It could be worse," she says.

"He is wearing a macramé vest and no shirt. Tell me how it could be worse."

"Ron could have sat the two of you together at the wedding."

"I'm not going."

"Damon," she says in a gentle reproach.

"Am I really a total basket case?" I ask.

"No, of course not. I haven't started setting you up with my geriatric friends yet, have I?"

"You are enjoying this!"

"Only slightly."

"Did Allan know about this set-up?"

"No, the punk is smarter than we think. He must have known Allan would have stopped him and didn't say a thing. He couldn't hold it in, though; he told CJ and me at the last minute. We figured we would try to keep the two of you separated for as long as possible. I thought after a few drinks you might be mellow enough that I could just tell you the truth and you wouldn't freak out and cause a scene."

"I guess I hadn't yet drunk enough."

"This will cheer you up. I have a pool going. When Allan gets the bonfire going, what will happen first: Johnny getting so wasted he accidentally falls into the flames or you purposely tossing in Ron?"

"The safe money is on the latter. By the time Allan gets the fire going, Johnny won't even be capable of walking, much less any form of leaping or diving that would get him into the flames."

"Actually, I'm still offering even odds."

"What happens if someone other than me throws Ron in the fire?"

"House loses, it has to be you. By the way, what is up with his art? At first I thought it was one of those paintings where they let an elephant pick up a brush with his trunk and splash paint on a canvas."

I giggle a little.

"Chin up, young man," she says, "this is only tragic if you get really drunk and go home with the guy Ron set you up with."

After dinner we gather in the front room for Allan to open his presents. It takes him a while to get to the package I brought. He starts to undo the wrapping.

"Allan," I say, "you've got to read the card first."

Allan stops ripping the paper and turns to the card. A folded piece of paper falls out of the envelope when he opens it. He unfolds it and starts to read to himself. He breakes into a wide grin.

"What is it?" asks Lucinda.

"Here, let me just read it aloud. So it is a print-out of an email Pickle sent to Damon. 'Dear Allan,' it says, 'I'm so bummed out I can't be there for the big day. I've heard a lot about your new digs and figured I could team up with Damon and CJ and Johnny to get you something for it and still be a part of everything even though I am so far away on the other side of the planet. I guess this needs to be an engagement gift too!!!! Damon had kept me filled in on everything. Anyway, Damon hatched this scheme over email. He wired me money for the gift, and I sent it back with Johnny and CJ when we met in Japan. There was originally a handwritten note, but those bitches lost it. I thought I could write you another card and mail it, but it would probably take months for the camels to carry it out of here and it would miss your birthday. Kisses. Pickle.'"

"Have you been emailing a lot?" Allan asks me.

"Yes, we've probably been talking more now than when he

lived here. His emails are astonishing. Do you know that most of the buildings in Ulaanbaatar are large tents, even though they are essentially permanent residences? The tents are ties back to their nomadic past."

Allan unwraps the gift. It is a rug; woven in Mongolia, what Pickle told me over the computer is a very traditional pattern. Allan rolls out the rug. He is obviously quite touched.

He opens a small box from Johnny and CJ next. It contains an irregular glass object. I can't make out what it is, but it reflects light in several primary colors.

Johnny explains how they are all over Japan right now. It is a dinosaur. They are in all the swankiest boutiques in Tokyo, he says.

The glass figure is passed around the room. It is indeed a crystal dinosaur: a tyrannosaurus with red claws and yellow spines running down its back. Allan puts it on the hearth after it makes its way around the room.

"It matches my painting so well," says Ron, "both in colors and in theme!" Apparently the painting has something to do with dinosaurs? Lucinda and I make the mistake of looking at each other and can barely contain our laughter. She nearly snorts some of her drink out her nose.

Travis comes over to me. This is the first time we talk since we got to the house.

"Nathan is getting a ride over here after their performance. Can you give both of us a ride back to my place after the party?"

I tell him it is no trouble.

People slowly filter out over the next hour. Hemp Guy leaves without comment. It is soon just my core group of friends. Nathan gets dropped off when Allan gets the bonfire going in the backyard. I stopped drinking a while ago to sober up for the drive home, so I pour myself some club soda with cranberry juice and a little lemon. Everyone else grabs some beer. Johnny and CJ, Seth and Lucinda, Travis and Nathan, Allan and Ron, and I sit around the fire. The breeze has kicked up enough that we all sit on the western side of the flames to keep out of the smoke. This is the first time almost everyone has met Nathan, so he gets asked all the same questions he got asked last weekend about living in Budapest and playing in the quartet. Other than a quick hug when Nathan arrives, he and Travis don't show much affection for one another, but everyone knows they are seeing each other.

CJ talks about his trip to Fuerteventura with *Surf/Trek*, and Lucinda tells us about her latest client, a good-natured but dotty retiree who wants a purple theme garden.

Nathan finishes his beer and asks if anyone else wants something from the kitchen. The empty bottles are piling up around the fire, so he gathers as many as he can and asks Allan where to discard them.

"I've just been putting them in the trash," responds Allan, motioning towards the cans that line the side of the garage.

Ron jumps up. "Are you telling me you haven't been putting them in the recycling?"

"I usually put glass in the recycling," says Allan, "but for the party I figured it would be OK to put bottles in the trash."

"But during a party is precisely the most important time to recycle." Ron is jumping up and down. "We need to set a good example for these people. And if you don't recycle when there are a lot of people around and there is a lot of waste, what is the point of recycling the rest of the time?"

Allan is standing now, too. "I thought maybe for my birthday I could just enjoy myself and let myself not stress about segregating the fucking trash."

"Well, I've got to stress about segregating the trash, since you're so busy worrying about such important things as whether it was a mistake to plant an even number of shrubs along the driveway rather than an odd number and whether we should dig them all up and replant them because you will always be looking out and wishing there were eleven rather than ten. Because of shit like that I've got to step up and take care of the day-to-day responsibilities like segregating the recycling."

"You need to shut up. You need to shut the fuck up," screams Allan. "This is my home, and if it wasn't for me you'd be living on the street, pushing your beloved empty bottles around in a shopping cart."

"I wasn't going to bring it up, but I saw you throw a magazine in the trash earlier, too. It was probably that *Men's Fitness* you've been looking at all the time and lusting after the model in the "Twelve Exercises for Ripped Abs" article that is running around the gym in nothing but skimpy shorts. You didn't recycle the magazine, and I'm not the abs model you wish I was. You didn't recycle the magazine right in front of my face, after I did all the cooking for your friends and even tried to find a date for your desperate, horny buddy."

"You fucking bitch, and this is all probably some fucking method acting exercise for your upcoming audition for *Fucking Bitchy-Ass Whiny Gay Man on a Hot Tin Roof* or some such thing. Fuck you."

I look around the circle. CJ is fixing the cuff of his jeans. Seth is giving Lucinda a neck massage. Johnny is pretty much comatose. Nathan is still standing with his arms full of empty bottles and looking from person to person in a total panic. Growing up, I had this one uncle who would signal the end of family dinners by leaning back in his chair, rubbing his belly, and saying "Well," stretching the monosyllable to unbelievable lengths. My aunt would fetch everyone's purses and jackets, say her good-byes, and we would all leave. Allan and Ron's fights combine that signal to depart with some elaborate foreplay. The incriminations, the shaming, the threats, the calculated transgressions all take on a greater impact before an audience.

Nathan understands none of this. Obviously Travis hasn't warned him. "Maybe we should go," he says. "I've had a busy day and could use some sleep." It is a rookie mistake. The rest of us know better than to make such a comment; it gives Allan and Ron the opportunity to pull you into their fight.

"See what you have done?" Allan wails at Ron. "We try to welcome people into our home, and you scare them away with your crazy shit and fucking explosive temper. Sit down and relax, Nathan.

My boyfriend doesn't mean anything by this display."

"Why blame me, you ass, when you're the one who can't recycle in front of company? I have to apologize, Nathan, that you have to see my boyfriend behaving this way."

"I need another club soda," I say as I get up. "I'll walk to the kitchen with you, Nathan. Let's just put the bottles down and let the boys take care of them latter."

"No, he is going to relax in front of the fire and chill out," screams Ron.

"We're not going to scare our friends away," adds Allan.

At least they seem to agree on this point. Nathan is stuck between them. I put my arm on his shoulder and guide him inside. I think I hear the Vietnam vet running back and forth along the fence as we go to the back door.

Nathan and I are standing in the kitchen. I explain to him that this is nothing out of the ordinary. I call Lucinda's cell phone. Out the window I see her get up and walk away from the fire to talk.

"Good god," she says, "if they can pull out all the stops like this for a birthday, can you imagine what the wedding will be like?"

"Ron will pull out the paddle and spank Allan right on the altar," I say. "It will be the photo-op social-conservatives salivate after. We need to go."

"I know. Seth and I were trying to decide if we should put out the fire before we leave. They're going to be at it as soon as we're out the door, and a fire this size shouldn't be left unattended."

"They're probably just going to fuck on the ground next to it. Round up the boys and meet Nathan and me out front."

We rendezvous on the front lawn. We can still hear screaming. They might be throwing stuff now. I'm sure the vet next door is beside himself in confusion.

6

THE SANTA ANNAS KICK IN the next week, and the basin fills with smog and hot inland air. Saturday morning I wake up cranky. It might be my allergies—I always get headaches in weather like this—or it might be that I allowed Travis to talk me into driving him and Nathan to Pick-N-Save for some shopping. I must have felt guilty for our spat last weekend; why else would I agree to this? How easily a trip to Pick-N-Save might spin out of control into a discount shopping orgy. I resolve to dump them both on the side of the freeway if they suggest dropping by Ross or Payless Shoes on the way home. In the shower it occurs to me I hadn't asked Travis why it was so urgent we go to Pick-N-Save. I'll ask in the car.

I go online while finishing my tea to search for the nearest Pick-N-Save. I scan the emails in my inbox: a Mongolia update from Pickle, a bunch of spam, and one from Russ asking if I want to go to the Bontecou exhibit at the Hammer with him. I've been meaning to go; I'll give him a call later. There is a Pick-N-Save just outside downtown in Korea Town, but I also find one on Colorado in Pasadena. During these inverted winds all the smog is blown out of the San Gabriel Valley; the mountains should be spectacular on a December day like today. If I'm stuck going to Pick-N-Save, I might as well get to see some blue sky. We could have lunch in Eagle Rock. Maybe we could hang out at Swork and get coffee. I might as well make this outing into something palatable.

I pick up Travis and Nathan and tell them about my plan to go to Pasadena. When we emerge from the tunnels near Dodger stadium on the 110 north, I see I was correct: the sky is so clear that Mt. Wilson appears to be about two meters away.

I turn to Travis and ask him why we are going to Pick-N-Save.

"I need some stuff for the loft."

"What kind of stuff?"

"Homey knickknacks."

"Homey knickknacks? I don't understand."

Nathan leans forward from the backseat to join the conversation. "It is because of a comment I made. Travis's loft feels very sterile, I said. I told Travis he doesn't need to do this, but he is insisting."

"I just want to make the place more comfortable for you."

Neither of them says anything for a long time.

I finally start talking to fill the silence, "I don't know that we will find a lot at Pick-N-Save to really transform your place. You know, we can go to Target afterward. They have some stuff that is stylish and affordable. I'm sure we can put something together. It's a positive thing to try to make your place more comfortable for your..." and I really don't know what word to use here. "Guy," I finally say. "It is a positive thing to make your place more comfortable for your guy." I like the sound of it.

"Well, you know," says Nathan, "I've also said on several occasions it would be nice to have sex with you, Travis, but you ignore me on that one. The knickknack comment, however, you latch on to."

I would have been better off enjoying the view than asking why we were making this trip. I am stunned. I try to think of something to say that might diffuse the tension, but Travis speaks up before I can think of anything.

"If you are so unhappy, why do you keep showing up at my place?" he says.

"Because you are super intelligent and I like listening to all the interesting things you have to say and you are one of the most handsome men I have ever met. But you can't pretend that sex isn't necessary."

"But it isn't. And we've been together in bed."

"You know that isn't sex."

"You had an orgasm."

"Shit! This is like being in high school."

Against my will, despite my attempts to lose myself in the liquid ambers changing colors on the hillsides and the rocking PJ

Harvey song on the stereo, I learn the following: Nathan and Travis have done nothing more than kissing each other, giving each other massages, and maybe mutual masturbation. Or it might just be that Nathan masturbated with Travis next to him—I don't ask for clarification. And the masturbation thing came after a lot of begging from Nathan. And Travis thinks he can clear all this up by buying pot holders and coasters at Pick-N-Save.

When we walk in the sliding-glass doors, the store smells as if there was some big drum in the back labeled "store scent" and small aliquots of this synthetic substance are aerosolized into the air conditioning at regular intervals to maintain this smell, the retail equivalent of bad cologne. Or possibly there is a twenty-foot-tall, scented cardboard pine-tree cutout, just a monster version of the ones designed to hang from rearview mirrors, hanging somewhere in the store. I look around. It could be concealed behind the mile-high stack of Spaghetti-O's. My job is too draining to waste my weekends like this.

Nathan and Travis get a cart, and I tell them that I'm going to look around the store and that they should come find me when they are done. I head in the opposite direction from them and find myself in the health-care aisle. The hemorrhoid-cream section is unbelievably large, as is the selection of antifungal foot creams and douches. So much shelf space dedicated to the more unsavory bodily functions.

Then the song on the sound system ends and "Midnight at the Oasis" comes on. This happens to be my all-time favorite cheesy

'70s easy listening guilty pleasure. There is nobody else in this aisle so I do a little dance move, rocking out to the piped-in tune, and find myself face to face with what must be three dozen different scents of bathroom spray.

I decide I have found my answer to the mystery of the store's smell. Maybe at the end of the day the employees choose an unlikely combination of these sprays (say, pumpkin, Irish glen, and sunshine spice) and set them off like flea bombs as they rush out the doors. They could maybe duct-tape the buttons down and sprint to escape the mingling fumes. The only thing that could make this moment better is if "Wichita Lineman" is the next song they play. Or maybe "Bette Davis Eyes." I'm ready to do more dancing when Nathan walks up the aisle towards me.

"I'm really sorry about all that in the car. You shouldn't have had to sit through that."

I just shrug. I don't want to talk about it anymore. I start walking down the aisle looking at the products on the shelf, but Nathan keeps walking with me.

"I'd like to make this up to you, not only for the car-ride argument but also for the trip to retail hell. Maybe tonight, if you don't already have plans—and I've already run this by Travis so he's OK with it—maybe we could get high. Just pot, nothing more. I don't do it often, because it starts messing with my concentration when I play, but I got these pot oatmeal-chocolate chip cookies from our cellist. I don't really want to try them alone. She warned me they are super-powerful."

This is something I used to do quite regularly. I knew I would have to take a drug test when I started my position, so I stopped six months before finishing graduate school and never started again. It felt like something I had outgrown. Nathan's offer, however, strikes me more like a reunion with an old friend. He's only in town for the weekend, you hang out, reminisce, maybe allow yourself to be goaded into something you usually wouldn't do, just to show off a bit and prove you haven't gotten too old, and then part and resume your separate lives. On the downside, I'm not eager to spend more time with these two.

Nathan and I have reached the end of the health products aisle and are about to round the display at the end of the aisle and enter the odd-shaped Tupperware section, when the glass figures in the display catch my eye: brontosauruses, triceratopses, stegosauruses, pterodactyls hanging from fishing-line loops, even a few tyrannosauruses—a veritable Jurassic menagerie.

"Nathan," I say, "it is the crystal T-Rex CJ and Johnny gave Ron for his birthday."

"I don't think I was there for that part."

"They made a big deal about how it was from Japan, and very fashionable there."

"So they're also imported here."

"No, they didn't buy the dinosaur in Japan, they got it here at Pick-N-Save."

"They'd lie about that?"

"Johnny would. This is too funny. That gift was made in a

Chinese sweatshop and purchased for ninety-nine cents at Pick-N-Save."

"Are you going to tell Johnny?"

"No, he'd die of embarrassment. But I might need to call Lucinda."

I see Travis across the store and motion him over. I hold out the glass T-Rex on my palm. He recognizes it immediately.

"This is scandalous," he says.

For a couple of minutes we make jokes about CJ and Johnny's scheme.

"So, Travis," I say, "Nathan says we're all going to get high tonight."

"I'm not going to do it. I said it wouldn't bother me if you two do. I'll bring a book. I've got to get caught up on some reading."

"Well," I say, "if we are going to do this, we have to do it at my place. It has to be somewhere comfortable, and we need some provisions. I'll look what tortilla chips they have here; I've got to have tortilla chips. I also saw some chili-lime peanuts in the snack section by the door; those sound good. And we need candles. I don't have any at my place, and I'm really into mellow lighting when I'm baked."

"They have candles here," says Travis.

"I don't want a condo full of Virgin Mary votives. We'll stop by Ikea or Pier-1 or something."

I buy a whole shopping bag full of junk food and still manage to get change back from a ten. Travis settles on a dozen assorted cacti in terra-cotta pots from the Pick-N-Save garden rack.

I decide to go to the Coffee Table in Eagle Rock because I need some heavy food in my stomach before we eat the cookies, and the Coffee Table has the best blue-cheese burger ever. And the french fries are always super crispy, right from the deep-fryer.

I don't need to look at the menu since I know exactly what I want, but Nathan and Travis need some time to make up their minds. I notice one of the guys bringing out food and busing the tables; he looks a little like the actor from *Donnie Darko*. He has the same dark, impossibly dense hair. And the perfect haircut: kind of messy, kind of spiky. Nathan finally decides on a protein salad, and Travis gets a tofu scramble.

We sit outside at one of the tables on the sidewalk. The couple at the next table has a fox terrier that suns itself and pants contentedly as he watches for interesting foot traffic along Colorado Boulevard. I lean back and pet the terrier.

"I was just thinking," says Travis. "I still have those little glass candleholders at my place that Lucinda brought over for the party. There is a whole unused bag of tea-lights. Would those work for you?"

"Actually, those would be perfect. And we have to go by your place anyway to get the cookies and drop off the cacti."

"Awesome, one less errand to run," says Nathan.

"Let's just stop by the grocery store. I don't have any semisweet chocolate chips at home. We definitely need those," I say.

Hair Guy himself brings us our food. I forget to ask him

for ketchup before he walks back to the kitchen. I'm here enough to know the ketchup is on a shelf in the upper room so I get up and fetch the bottle myself. As I go inside, I run right into Hair Guy walking back to our table with some ketchup.

"Sorry about that," he says.

"No problem, I was just going to grab a bottle myself."

"You didn't think I'd forget. You can't have fries without ketchup."

"You're totally right."

"And your friend might want some for his eggs."

"Not unless Heinz is now all organic."

"I should have known. The tofu-scramble people never know how to live."

"As opposed to the burger-and-fries people."

"Exactly. Except you obviously don't eat burgers and fries all the time."

"You haven't worked here long, have you? I don't remember seeing you before."

"I used to work in the Silver Lake location. You don't go to Silver Lake much?"

"I do, but I always eat at that Vietnamese place on Sunset that I don't know the name of because it doesn't even have a sign. Obviously, it isn't somewhere I could take tofu scramble and protein salad."

"I love that place. We should go sometime." He pauses to see if I'll take him up on the offer. I can't contain my broad smile.

"Good," says Hair Guy. "I'll drop my number at your table before you go." And he turns and walks back to the kitchen.

He does exactly what he said and gives me his number on a napkin while we are eating. I'm just as pleased as anything.

Nathan and Travis wait in the car when I go into Vons to buy chocolate chips. I get two bags and go to the checkout, getting behind a father and his high school-age son in the shortest line. The father has his gray hair pulled back in a ponytail and wears a plain T-shirt, worn jeans, and soiled tennis shoes.

"There's no need to put the milk into bags," he yells forward to the box-boy, referring to four one-gallon bottles. The men live alone judging from the groceries: a flat of ramen noodles, economy boxes of cereal, bunches of bananas, and two pieces of cake from the bakery. Looking at the pieces of cake, I imagine that one of them is having a birthday, and this is their celebration.

The son is distracted by a sports magazine while the father unloads the last of the groceries from the cart. A flat of soda is lodged under the foldout seat in which one can place small children. The flat is giving him some trouble to unload. I reach down, grab it, and help him lift it onto the checkout stand.

"Thanks for the hand," he says jovially. "I should be in better shape…it might help with the ladies, too."

The son, all awkward and acne-faced, puts the magazine in front of his old man, points to one of the pages, and mutters something I can't catch. The two of them laugh and turn away from me, the man to pay the ruddy cashier and the boy to return the magazine to the rack.

It is dark by the time we get to my apartment. We light the candles and eat the cookies. Travis keeps a table lamp on so he can read his book. An hour passes and I wonder if the cookies will ever kick in. Nathan keeps admiring my place and telling me how comfortable it is, trying all the chairs and the couch like a floppy dog deciding where to settle for a nap. I put on a Nina Simone album, since I know most people don't like the indie rock I listen to.

I think the cookies are just going to do nothing. I straighten up magazines. I switch to Ella Fitzgerald singing Duke Ellington after Nina Simone ends. Halfway through "Don't Get Around Much Anymore," as I am singing along with Ella and dancing around the room, I realize I'm not quite acting normally. Nathan is laughing at me and appears to be struggling not to fall off the couch. Travis keeps reading and ignores us. I just kill on "Satin Doll."

Nathan is going through my CDs. "My first love back in London was an indie rock fan, too," he says. He seems to be lost in thought for a minute. "You know, you reminded me of Jacob from the first time I met you. He was quiet and intense, like you."

"What happened?"

"You are just such an idiot when you're nineteen. You have this wonderful guy who will dance around the living room with you and stay up reading poetry to you, and you are sure the world is full of better, greater things. Then, when it is too late, you realize how, more than anything, you just want to go back to what you once had."

He scans the CDs and grabs one and puts it in the machine. It is Massive Attack, "Protection."

He grabs my hand and pulls me up from the floor. He puts his hand on my butt and pulls me in to him.

"You can really dance, Damon."

"I love this song, too," I say.

Nathan spins me as we grow more comfortable together. Then he does it again, but only half a twirl, and pulls me backwards in to him and holds my waist.

"I've never understood the 'I'm a girl, I'm a boy' part," he says, "but it is so terribly sexy when Tracy Thorn sings it."

I turn to face him again and lean my head against his neck and close my eyes. His hand rubs up and down my back, and we stay that way until the song ends.

Then I feel like I can't do anything other than change to a Shins album and lie on my back on the floor. Nathan goes and bugs Travis who is still trying to read.

I think about "Protection" which makes me think about how John Cusack names it one of his five top side-one, track-ones of all time in *High Fidelity*, which makes me want to listen to "Dry the Rain," but I only have that on my iPod which is down in the car.

I think about the guys that Prada has been using in its magazine advertisements over the last few months, who are just so hot. I want to crawl over to the coffee table to get a *GQ* so I can find one of the ads and just look at it for a while. The models are vaguely central European: heavy eyebrows, full lips, none of those delicate

WASP noses. This makes me think of leafy summer parks—some image of Prague or Munich I've picked up over the years, children frolicking with helium balloons, guiding boats in ponds, watching puppet shows. I think of marionettes, which makes me think of the beginning of *Being John Malkovich*, which is, obviously, another movie with John Cusack. But I was just thinking of John Cusack in *High Fidelity*, so it seems of utmost significance that two different trains of thought converge on John Cusack. I contemplate John Cusack. Either two hours or about ten minutes pass. Nathan is munching his way through the bag of food from Pick-N-Save, so I have him toss me the chili peanuts. Nathan has his shirt off and is trying to get Travis to give him a massage. I tell them they can spend the night in my spare bedroom, and then I notice they are gone and I assume that is where they went.

I had forgotten how different some music sounds when you are high: lyrics that sound muddled when you are sober become well articulated, fuzzy chords expand into dioramas. My hand over my own chest is electric. I wish I had invited Hair Guy over tonight. I can't decide if I should go to the kitchen for chocolate chips, change the album, or masturbate. So much makes sense right now. No one may ever have this same knowledge again.

7

MY LAB IS CLOSED BETWEEN CHRISTMAS AND NEW YEAR'S, so after spending Christmas at my mom's, I fly to New York for a week and get a room ay my favorite Chelsea hotel. I'm blown away by one of Tomasetti's works at the Whitney—from across the gallery you see luminous garlands painted on a black background, all these colorful inverted arcs that hang from the top edge of the canvas. When you get close you see the canvas is Plexiglas and the garlands are not paint, but linear collages glued on the Plexiglas. One garland may be all illustrations of birds, another might be illustrations of flowers, and many are chains of what appear to be real pharmaceuticals. The artist seemed to want to simultaneously make a striking pattern and to catalog the world. I can't figure out how he created the black void behind the Plexiglas.

By the time I get back to Los Angeles, Nathan and Travis have moved into my spare bedroom. Nathan says it is more convenient to the quartet's practice space (which really isn't true) and it is more cozy than Travis' loft (which is true) and that Travis doesn't really care where they stay (he did once live in a pickup, after all) and that I did give them a key and told them they could hang out whenever they wanted (which is true, except "hang out" and "move in" are not synonyms).

I quickly grow accustomed to living with other people again. I welcome having others with whom to eat dinner and watch TV on those nights when I'm too tired to go to the gym. We start developing our own dumb inside jokes. From a *Simpsons* episode we start saying, "I am so smart, I am so smart," over and over in a lilting voice every time we do something intelligent but insignificant—like getting an extra bowl in which to place the pistachio shells rather than letting them fall off the paper towel and onto the couch, or hitting the pause button on the remote when someone gets up to use the bathroom in the middle of watching a DVD. We find this hilarious.

Travis is often sleeping on the couch when I get up in the morning. I assume it is part of their unconventional sexual relationship and do not ask more about it. One night, however, during a particularly trying week at work, I wake up around 3:00 in the morning and can't get back to sleep. I get up to get a glass of water and find Travis sitting up awake in an armchair, wrapped in a quilt and staring out the window.

"Nightmares," he says.

He had these all the time when we were roommates in college; I assumed he had outgrown them sometime in the intervening years.

107

He sleeps on the couch so he doesn't keep waking up Nathan.

"The worst part," he says, "is that any part of a nightmare is part of you. It is in your brain, not projected from the outside like a movie. The worst part is that such images can be created by you."

Nathan is constantly shirtless or, more often, just in a pair of briefs. He looks like he belongs on the outside of a Calvin Klein underwear box. I find my mind drifting back to images of him throughout the day. He does manage to pull on a shirt when we sit at the table and eat dinner.

Denise calls Friday afternoon to see if I want to meet this weekend.

"Why the fuck haven't I heard from you?" she says. "Let's have lunch on Sunday. I've got something I want to run by you; I'm thinking about buying a bigger set of tits. Let's meet at Ciudad at 2:00. Does that work for you?"

"Sure, I've got a date Sunday night."

"Great, give the boob conundrum some thought."

After our conversation on the phone I'm sure the breast implants are the first thing she'll want to talk about when we get our table, but we start by chatting about other things.

"How's Travis?" she says. "I know this kind of shit is the most awkward, so we should just get it out of the way. And don't think you have to lie about stuff because of my feelings. I'm a big girl."

"He's dating a guy."

"I told you, didn't I? And you thought I was crazy."

"They're over at my place all the time. His boyfriend is a

great guy. A classical musician, really good looking."

"Over at your place?"

"Yah, they stay in my spare room most of the time."

"This doesn't bother you?"

"I guess I missed the company. Do you ever go out dancing? We should go out, it might be fun."

"I do go clubbing now and then. Gay clubs are so much more fun. I hate the predatory shit you have to deal with around drunk hetero guys."

"A bunch of us are going to Drag Strip next month. We've been trying to go for months but keep missing it. It is organized by drag queens, but you can totally go and not dress up. There is always some sort of theme: Bollywood, *Golden Girls* versus *Facts of Life*, Under the Sea…and all the drag queens try to dress to match the theme. Even those of us who don't do drag wore sarongs for Under the Sea."

"Sounds good. Let's just remember to give Travis a heads-up. When is it and what's the theme?"

"Second Saturday of the month. The theme is "Paleolithic-a-go-go: cave queens, dino-divas, Jurassic cosmetology."

"But the Jurassic and the Paleolithic have nothing to do with each other."

"I told you, it is organized by drag queens, not Stephen J. Gould."

"My god," says Denise, "what is up with that annoying friend of yours. Have you punched him yet?"

"Ron? I haven't seen him for a few weeks, not since this party at his boyfriend's place." I tell her about the party: about Ron and Allan fighting in front of all of us and scaring Nathan and about the crystal T-Rex from Pick-N-Save that was supposed to be the hot gift from Japan.

"You've got to call Johnny and CJ on that shit. That is hilarious."

"No," I say, "I'm not trying to stir up trouble."

"You've got no balls."

"Weren't we going to talk about breasts?" I say.

"Here is the thing, Damon: I've got to stop dating homos. I know why you guys love me: I'm a bitch, I'm raunchy, and I've got great shoes. But Damon, I want to be fucked, not worshipped. So I need to reach out to that other demographic. My tits...are obviously not by best asset. Straight men like tits, I don't have tits, ergo I've got to get me a pair. But is it safe? That's what I want to talk to you about."

"You really should be talking to a doctor. I'm not really up on the biomaterials side of things. But from what I know, I'd be wary. I believe, even with the best implants, they need to be redone every decade or so. You need to check on that. In risk analysis you have to factor in two things: the probability that something might go wrong and the gravity of the problem if it does. So a doctor might tell you they are 99.9 percent safe. But there is that 0.1 percent left over. You don't want something going wrong with your body. It is not a car where you can just replace a part—you disrupt the balance, and things could go wrong anywhere."

"I really need the breasts, though."

"Let me go at this another way. Have you tested your theory? Will big breasts really change anything for you?"

"There is no test-driving breast implants."

"But aren't there really good padded bras out there? Hell, my friend CJ I told you about is a drag queen, I'm sure he could hook you up. Maybe you need to get a pair of falsies, go out to a club, and see what the response is. Maybe the breast thing is not as big a deal as you think."

Denise and I chat for another hour, but I don't eat much since Hair Guy and I are going to the no-name Vietnamese restaurant. I soon wish I had suggested a movie rather than dinner, since Hair Guy seems to have both ADD and industrial-grade loquaciousness. Dinner is him performing a monologue. It is so bad I even consider making some lame excuse to end the date and not even bother trying to get him into bed. There is a brief pause in his talking when he starts choking on a hunk of beef from his pho. In the instant before he hacks up the gobbet of meat I have my break; I can say some fib about having to go over to my mom's house to help change a lightbulb and prematurely end this date. What comes out of my mouth, however, is not the lie:

"After dinner do you want to go to my place?" I say. He is, after all, very hot.

Unfortunately, Travis and Nathan are sitting on the couch watching a TiVo'd *Alias* when we get to my apartment. Special

Agent Damon tries to usher Hair past the surveillance on the couch quickly and nonverbally, but Travis hits pause and asks Hair how he liked dinner. And with a new audience the talking resumes, kicked up to a whole new level.

I get myself a glass of water, and Hair Guy is seated between Travis and Nathan on the couch, telling them about where he lives.

"It is like a total ghetto apartment, but it is walking distance to work, so I love it. A lot of culinary students from the school in Pasadena live there, and a few crazies. The guy downstairs from me never leaves his apartment; he just listens to his TV super loud and screams at people walking by his window through the blinds. It is really freaky, because he is right there but you can't see him. I've only seen downstairs freak outside his apartment a few times. He is totally bleached and pale. It is especially ironic because the guy in the apartment next to me is really into sunless tanning; he's tangerine-colored, just like those iron-age bog mummies they dig up in Scotland. But the insane part is that downstairs freak is also a racist and screams the N-word—if you can believe that—every time bog-mummy guy walks by, even though bog mummy is a Jew from Jersey, and who has ever seen a radiant orange black guy? So this new crazy guy just moved into the building. I didn't know he was crazy at first, I just thought he spent a lot of time walking around talking on his wireless headset, I mean, we don't really get reception inside our apartments—my theory is the layers and layers of lead paint block out the phone signal. Anyway, I was talking to another neighbor in the building, I can never remember her name, and it

112

has gotten to the point where we've talked too much for me to ask now without it getting awkward. She's a bitter divorcée so let's just call her Bitter Divorcée. Bitter Divorcée told me that if you listen to crazy phone freak as you walk by, he is not really talking on the phone but cussing you out. 'Kiss my ass, you wank,' he always says to me now that I know to listen. But you see, phone freak is black. Did I already say that? So we have a building betting pool going on how long it will take for a crazy-person smack-down face-off to occur. We figure one day phone freak will walk by downstairs freak's window, and downstairs freak will start with his racial slur thing, and the phone freak will just go off on racist downstairs freak, yelling his own obscenities into his cell phone and it will just escalate from there. Phone freak might get thrown out of the building before that happens because he showed up on Bitter Divorcée's doorstep wearing a Catholic schoolgirl's uniform asking her to photograph him. Our landlord was pissed. Apparently you can be too crazy even for our building."

Then Hair Guy sees the book Travis has been reading. "You won't believe this," he says, "I think God talked to me in a dream a few weeks ago." Nathan looks at me and rolls his eyes; Travis tries to look intently interested.

"So I was in the desert, with a reservoir on one side of me and these steep mountains on the other side. The ground was barren rock and very smooth and rose almost a perfect forty-five–degree grade to the top of the hills. On the shore of the reservoir were all these people dressed in old-fashioned clothes, like loose-fitting robes and cloth over their heads, they were gathering something—like clams or kelp, I didn't see what it was—from the shore of the reservoir. Anyway, in the dream I knew the people represented everyone on the planet, and this barren desert represented the world…but it gets even stranger! By the way, I'm really not too into the desert; you know I grew up in Albuquerque. I go back a few times a year. The best part is going for long runs in the good mountain air. The last time I went home, though, my brother gave me this long lecture about how I wasn't rehydrating carefully enough. I was so upset about his shit that I stayed home that night rather than going out with my high school friends and sat with my guitar and wrote a song about it. Do you have a guitar? I'd totally play it for you. Here in LA I don't run much outside because the smog gets to me; I mainly just use the treadmills and stair climbers inside at the gym. It is so funny, there is this guy at work, he's huge and all muscles, I used to see him at the gym all the time but then he just disappeared. He told me he started going to the 24 Hour Fitness in East Pasadena. I figured he started going there because it is less crowded—because it is—but he told me the reason is because it is next to Chuck E. Cheese. Now I know he wouldn't be eating there, because he is one of those guys who is all about his skinned chicken breasts and cottage cheese and keeps count of his protein intake on a pad in his back pocket, but he told me he gets so bored doing cardio at the gym that he has switched to doing an hour of Dance Revolution—that arcade game where you do the moves on the screen and hit the patches that light up on the floor with your feet—at Chuck E. Cheese before his workout. And I can't believe it, because he is the most serious guy and never even laughs, and he is at Chuck E. Cheese three nights a week dancing in front of all these kids. Anyway, the dream…I was standing on the shore of the reservoir in the desert, when God appeared to me—I've never had a dream with God in it before, so this really shook me up. And God wasn't the nice old man you see in paintings…God was like eight feet tall and super buff and really tan, with long black hair he kept in a ponytail. And he wore this crazy outfit that was sort of beads and leather and showed a lot of skin…maybe like an Egyptian/Native American/S&M sort of outfit. So God was very imposing, had strange fashion sense, and was generally stern and condescending in tone. I was scared but stood my ground and talked with him…and God was in the mood to talk of heresies. He told me I had successfully resisted the first heresy he had given the world to test our faith. What was the heresy? Well, Jesus. Apparently, he was made up by God to see who would actually fall for it, and God was pissed at those people who had. So, obviously my subconscious has some difficulty with Christianity. I try to be really accepting of all religions, you know, but I'm just not so comfortable with Christianity. It is like this one time I went on this date with a guy and I walked into his apartment, and the unholy trinity of dating deal-breakers were lined up on his living-room bookshelf: the Bible, some Alcoholics Anonymous book, and a DVD of every Disney movie ever made, like even the real obscure direct-to-video sequels and threequels. Anyway, then God warned me he was about to unleash a second heresy that was going to be an even bigger test for the world, that would potentially cause more deaths and wars than the Jesus heresy. And this heresy was going to fall from the sky—literally, like a falling satellite—sometime soon. Then God showed me what the heresy would look like...he made something like a short pillar, about two meters tall, appear, and on the top was the symbol of the heresy. But as soon as God made the heresy-pillar thing appear, he also caused this great disruption before I could get a good look at the symbol. I looked up, and there was this water that started pouring over the mountain. It was a great wave, a great flood, which fell down the mountain and swept me and all the people into the reservoir. I was getting tumbled around by the water, with all these people in robes around me, trying to find the surface, when I woke up. After I woke up from the dream, I was so agitated I had to get up and make myself a snack. When I used to train for marathons, my metabolism was so high I couldn't make it through the night without eating. I'd sleepwalk to the kitchen and make myself a sandwich and not even remember it happened when I woke up, until I rolled over and there would be a half-eaten turkey on sourdough in bed right next to me. It happened so frequently I just started making a sandwich each night before I went to bed and left it on my dresser so I wouldn't have to sleepwalk to the kitchen. I would always cut off the crust, since that was the part I wouldn't eat in my sleep and find in the morning in my sheets. And for a while I got into oranges rather than sandwiches and would wake up to find peels in my bed. Except I once heard about a guy who had a stroke that caused him to think he smelled oranges. So, when I woke with the orange peels in my bed, I would panic because the scent of them would cause me to think I was having a stroke, and I would have to convince myself otherwise…"

Travis says, "Smile, put your hands up, and repeat this simple phrase," quoting the stroke diagnosis questions from Lucinda and Seth's Christmas card. Unfortunately, I just took a drink of water, and Travis's comment catches me so off guard that I laugh uncontrollably and spray water clear over to the couch where it hits Hair, and he stops talking. The stunned look on Hair Guy's face makes Nathan laugh. Even Travis cracks a grin.

"So I am just a joke to you all, the hot dumb guy you will all make fun of in the morning when I'm gone," says Hair.

I start to explain about our silly little running joke, talking about the Christmas card, when I look over at Nathan and we again start laughing uncontrollably.

"Look, I've gotten this all my life," he says. "Yes, I like to talk. But fuck you, at least I don't invite guys home and then sit around with my roommates and make fun of them. Fuck you, I may not be as smart as all of you—I could barely get through high school since I was getting in trouble with the teachers for talking all the time—but fuck you. I'm leaving. And don't think I want a ride home from you, you stupid old fuck. I'll get a cab. Fuck you."

And he got up and left.

We all get quiet, and I feel really bad. And I feel really, really horny and needed this. Then I look at Nathan, and he is trying so hard not to laugh that tears are coming out of his eyes. I bust up all

117

over again.

8

"THERE WAS THIS ONE WINTER," says Seth, "when it never stopped raining. It must have been '95, if that was an El Niño year. It rained something like every day in March; it was a record in Sacramento for the most consecutive days of rain. You got the impression that all the attempts to control the water—the aqueducts and levees, the dams and pumping stations—just managed to barely restrain it below the surface most of the time, the water just waiting for the system to falter (as it did that winter) so that the inland sea might again rise up and reassert itself."

We are walking around a most unlikely Japanese garden in the Sepulveda basin. Seth and Lucinda wanted to visit it and picked me up on their way to the San Fernando Valley. Lucinda is sketching the dry garden in one corner—the raked gravel, the purposeful placement of the stones—while Seth and I walk the periphery of the lake in the main garden. Seth is unusually chatty.

119

"The Central Valley really is an inland sea, or it was before we tamed it," Seth continues. "It seems unlikely when we think about it now, but it used to flood every winter and become a vast wetland. It was once a Serengeti between the Sierra Nevada and the Costal Range. There are still a few sloughs that are protected, remnants of what the Central Valley once was. That rainy winter you glimpsed the Central Valley's true nature. The causeway was so flooded, Sacto looked like a waterfront city as you headed towards it on Interstate 80. When the rains finally broke, I was so eager to get back on my bike that I started out before the waters had fully receded. There was this one place in particular I remember: the field on one side of the road was flooded and draining over the asphalt in a thin sheet into a lower field on the opposite side of the road. The coat of water on the road was just thin enough to ride through, maybe an inch in depth. I felt like I was bicycling over the water itself. That spring I saw whole uprooted redwoods swept down the American River in the surge of water from the melting snowcaps."

The garden has gotten Seth talking about water because it was built in conjunction with an adjoining treatment plant to showcase the use of reclaimed waste water. A lake sits in the center of the garden, large enough to have several streams and waterfalls feeding it. The lake even has islands that must have symbolized one thing or another, islands complete with pines trimmed into poodle cuts. Dr. Koichi Kawana, famous in the Japanese-garden circuit, according to Lucinda, designed the garden back in the '80s.

"I first started cycling when I lived in Davis, and it hasn't been the same here in Los Angeles. The routes I take in Palos Verdes are beautiful, but up north I didn't even have routes. Outside of town I could just choose a direction and ride, turning left at a particular crossroads one day, right at the crossroads the next, exploring as much as I was cycling. My mind went feral. Snowy egrets would pause from their migrations in the rice fields, and I would imagine myself one of them if I was wearing my long-sleeved white jersey. From a small rural airport parachuters would practice on weekends, people in different-colored jumpsuits and chutes, tumbling from the sky in a long column, like Jacob's ladder. One spring I got a flat and stopped in an almond orchard to change my tube; the trees were blooming and the breeze caused the petals to fall about me, fluttering down like snowflakes."

Seth and I walk over a set of planks, a low bridge that zigzags in right angles across a pool planted with irises. I have never seen the bulbs growing submerged like this, tubers below the waterline.

"It was a painful time for me, yet beautiful, too. I lived on the edge of town. That apartment on the city limits suited me at the time. There were fields on three sides of the apartment complex, a convenience store and an empty lot across the street. My stark room contained only white walls, a futon, my bike, pale carpet, and a tape player plugged into an electrical socket. My window looked over the fields, those flat Sacramento Valley fields that stretch unblocked to the north, to the horizon. In that empty lot across the street, every summer the heat created dust devils which sucked litter high above the ground. Every autumn there was one evening when the moon appeared twice its normal size and floated right above the horizon at dusk, making everything glow a stagnant lavender. One week every spring the spiders hatched and escaped into the air on silk streamers more plentiful than the stars, and every winter there was one night when the fog descended and the atmosphere became moist, and a slight breeze would hit your cheek, and you would swear you were back home on the beach."

The garden hugs an administrative building, futuristic in design, a bold yet apt choice to complement a traditional garden. Seth leads me to a stairway, and we climb to an observation platform jutting outward from the administration building's third floor. Most of the deck overlooks the garden, but from one corner you can view the processing plant on the far side of the wall enclosing the garden. Metal catwalks overlay an array of rectangular pools—scores of them—dark and frothy.

"You probably know what all this is," says Seth.

"They're pools where bacteria digest sewage. You need the bubbling for the bacteria to get oxygen. They break down the waste, bit by bit, the solids digested as they flow from one side of the pool to the other, falling to the bottom of the sloped floor at the pool's far end, the sludge pumped off the bottom away to another facility to make fertilizer. This is the whole reason the garden is here, isn't it?" I say.

Seth and I walk back to the opposite side of the observation deck for a more scenic view. We lean against the railing. The garden is constructed like an ancient walled city: verdant inside, an oasis, a refuge—protected from the desert without. Standing at ground level in the garden, bamboo or ginkgo or decorative stonework obscures the walls and distorts your perspective, increasing subliminally your sense of protection within. Only from this vantage on the observation deck do you appreciate the garden's artful manipulation of your senses.

"I was terribly promiscuous those days back in Davis," says Seth. "I hardly spoke to anyone—family or friends—not, at least, about anything important. And I was alone so much, on my bike or drinking. Sex was the only way to connect; it was my only open line of communication. I'm sure the girls thought they'd save the brooding, taciturn cyclist. For me, it was the only way I could express tenderness or even interest in another person. I couldn't handle normal conversation then. There was just so much junk—my lies, my imploding self, my raging anger—not to mention the insufferable games and role-playing you can never escape at that age. Sex was the only way to cut through it all."

For a moment I think this speech by Seth must be something Lucinda put him up to, although that would certainly not be Lucinda's style. Maybe all the talk of floods and cycling in Davis was a prelude to working his way to the real subject of promiscuity. I think, however, that it is really just Seth talking, maybe in the mood to reminisce, maybe showing concern in a sideways manner about my own wayward sex life that seems to have everybody upset but myself. I've worked with a lot of straight men over the years, and I've had several friendships where I'm surprised by the frankness of the conversations they have with me.

Lucinda walks towards us across the garden, waving.

"Obviously, she'd never fall for the man-who-needs-saving delusion," says Seth. "You know she wouldn't stand for that for a moment."

Lucinda ascends the stairs and joins us on the observation deck.

"Isn't this all wonderful?" Lucinda gestures with a sweep of her arm toward the garden. "What time do we have to get you home?"

"Around six," I say.

"It is so nice for Travis and Nathan to come over and make you dinner. Nathan is cooking, I hope," she says.

"Some Hungarian food, I think."

"He and Travis seem really good together, do you see them often?" asks Seth.

"Now and then," I say.

Lucinda offers to buy us tea and snacks at the tea house on the lake. "I know it is cheesy," she says, "but I just love it."

I don't eat anything other than the snacks from the tea house for the rest of the afternoon and am so famished by the time Nathan gets his meal on the table that I just attack the food: heavy, like everything else I've tasted from Central Europe, but also spicy and tasty—without any German or Polish blandness—and glowing red with paprika. Travis picks at his boiled potatoes. He talks to Nathan about the works the quartet is practicing. More talk of Bartók while

I eat my second bowl of goulash soup, soup Nathan ladled for me without even asking if I wanted seconds when he saw me wiping the first bowl clean with a hunk of buttered bread.

Travis asks about Liszt as I gnaw meat from the bones of some paprika chicken.

"He was more of a piano composer, no real place in the string-quartet repertoire," says Nathan, "and he wasn't really even Hungarian. Not that we only play Hungarian composers, by any means. Liszt was Austrian born but moved to Budapest when young; he was maybe even a Magyar in his heart, but he never learned to speak the language. There is much of this, really: non-Hungarians falling in love with the country and adopting it. Magyarphiles should be the word. Elizabeth Hapsburg was the most famous and the most beloved, and unlike Liszt she could speak the language perfectly."

I poured myself another glass of wine. The mention of Elizabeth stirred some recollection. "Wasn't she beautiful?" I say. "And didn't she have an affair with a Hungarian?"

"It was nothing tawdry." says Nathan. "It wasn't a consummated affair. You are talking about Andrássy. They were certainly in love—if it is possible to make that judgment about two people without being in their heads. She was an empress and he was an ambassador, so they were together in court, a formalized environment that would preclude any physical relationship. Her ability to speak Hungarian (she insisted she learn it rather than Czech) did allow them to hide in plain sight in the Hapsburg court. The Hungarians were the people next door, but their tongue was unintelligible, something wild, to the

Austrians. Elizabeth and Andrássy could converse in court in total privacy."

"So they could flirt with each other without the Austrians catching on," I say. This is more interesting than the talk of Liszt and Bartók.

"It was probably closer to platonic love than the high school crush you are imagining," says Nathan. "Some credit the relationship of Elizabeth and Andrássy with paving the way for the compromise, the formation of the dual monarchy in 1867. Elizabeth certainly did entreat her husband, Franz Hapsburg, to negotiate with the Hungarians, but it is debatable how important that influence was on Franz's decision to pursue the compromise. There was great pressure, without Elizabeth, for the emperor to reconcile with the Hungarians."

"What sort of emperor gives away power?" I ask. "Why compromise?"

"The Hapsburgs were an occupying nation, and such an occupation is never tenable in the long run. The Hungarians had already revolted once, in 1848. In that revolution they succeeded in breaking free; the Hapsburgs were in decline and didn't have the military to placate them. The Russians, however, did. The Hapsburgs called on their allies, and it was the Russians that squashed the revolution. The Austrians took back control and treated the Hungarians brutally for the following decades, treated them so badly that another revolt was imminent with simmering Hungarian dissatisfaction. The Hapsburgs couldn't stop a second revolution.

That is why they needed the compromise. They couldn't call on the Russians a second time. The Russians had asked for help from the Austrians during their war in the Crimea in reciprocation for their assistance in Hungary, and the Austrians had done nothing. The Russians weren't going to ride in and save the Austrians. A second Hungarian revolution would succeed, and the Hapsburgs would lose half their lands without the compromise. The Hungarians, however, could not just break free; they still needed the clout of the Austrians, even if it had diminished. They had a Russian empire to the east, ever ready to expand. Break with the Austrians, and they'd just end up dominated by a different empire. In the end, the whole compromise lasted a short time—only fifty years of dual monarchy before the Great War shattered everything. Ironically, it was the Hapsburg treatment of the Slavs rather than the Hungarians that doomed the venture."

Travis puts down his silverware and says, "I think it would be a good idea if you two started sleeping together."

Elizabeth Hapsburg is forgotten. I look back and forth between Nathan and Travis.

Nathan finally speaks. "What are you talking about, Travis? Are you breaking up with me?"

"No. Not at all. I think it would be good for our relationship if you two have sex. Damon would obviously be up for it. We can't go on like this—you'll either break up with me or cheat on me, as things stand. You two having sex is an arrangement that would please all of us."

"Is this about Damon and me dancing in front of you that one night? I know it was a little too intimate, but I was totally baked."

"I'm never going to have sex with you like you want," says Travis.

"This is insane," says Nathan.

"I know you need this, Nathan."

"Wait!" I say. "Don't I have a say in this?"

I am ignored. Travis tells Nathan about how much he cares about him and how unimportant sex is to him. "I just need honesty," he says, "I just don't want any lies."

Nathan asks Travis if he really thinks such an arrangement is realistic. "Do you think you could let me carry on with another guy—your good friend, at that—right in front of you without any jealousy?"

"There is no question I can." Travis stands up. "Dinner was great. I love potatoes. I'm heading home and don't want you to follow. I'm spending the night in my loft. I won't open the door if you knock; I won't answer the phone if you call. Spend the night here. I'll be back tomorrow morning." From another person, such a speech would be melodramatic. From Travis, the delivery is detached and analytical. He might have been me delivering a talk about rheology. Travis takes a coat from the spare bedroom and walks out my front door. Nathan and I are alone at the table.

We avoid each other's eyes.

"Maybe he is right," says Nathan, finally.

I can not believe I am hearing any of this and am quite shaken up. I tell Nathan that after we clean up the dishes we will just watch a DVD and he will sleep in the guest room as usual. To my surprise, Nathan keeps talking about Travis's proposition. He tells me that Travis certainly can deal with the two of us having sex if he says he can.

I am incredulous. "If I didn't know Travis's obsession with honesty, I'd guess the two of you had this planned. You'll be leaving by summer. You won't have to live with the repercussions of any of this," I say.

"How about this…if Travis still feels the same way tomorrow, at least say you'll consider it."

"Let's clean up the table," I say. I'm shaking a little, though, and Nathan notices. He asks if I want a cigarette. I rarely smoke, but I need a cigarette now to calm my nerves. I tell Nathan I'll meet him on the balcony and pour two gin and tonics before going outside.

"*Köszönöm szépen*," he says as he takes the drink.

I take a cigarette out of his pack, and he lights it for me. I look at him quizzically and ask him what he just said. I feel heady with the first inhalation of the smoke.

"'Thank you a lot,' I said. *Nagyon szépen köszönöm* would be more appropriate, 'thank you very much.' I really needed the drink."

"Was it hard to learn to speak Hungarian?"

"Impossible. The logic is so foreign. A noun can decline into something like twenty different cases. And the word order is variable. I always feel like I am shouting words randomly."

"It doesn't sound pleasant," I say as I sip my drink.

"But the language is beautiful. Words feel closer to their origin than in English. In a single generation the Magyar transformed from a band of seminomadic Siberian horsemen to a fully settled medieval European nation. Perhaps that abrupt transformation flash-froze the language before bureaucratization could denature their words."

Nathan looks at me. "*Gyümölcs*," he says. "Just listen to that word."

"How do you even spell that?" I ask.

"It is unimportant. Just listen—*gyümölcs*—it is the word for 'fruit.' The word itself is juicy and fleshy in your mouth." Nathan smiles for the first time since Travis's pronouncement. He continues, "It is just like taking a mouthful of the fullest summer peach. And *tyúk*, just say it over and over again: *tyúk, tyúk, tyúk*. It is the word for 'hen.' You say the word, and plump fowl are clucking at your feet. *Erős*—'strong'—you can hear the force in that second, long vowel."

Before I met my ex-boyfriend I dated this graduate student for a while. I think he studied archeology. On our second date he took me to his home, a guest-house in Atwater. We sat on his couch, taking drinks from beer bottles and kissing each other, stripping away our clothes. We went to his bedroom when the couch became restrictive. I was lying on his bed and thought he was going to blow me, when he pushed my legs over my body, put his face in my ass, and started rimming me. It was the first time anybody had eaten out my ass. I felt like I was losing my virginity all over again: it wasn't choreographed, but messy and thrilling and beyond what I imagined. I don't think I even realized that particular act was part of the repertoire before that night. I had no idea what might happen next.

Tonight with Nathan feels much the same. Maybe it is the disorientation because he says nothing in English, just giving names to my body parts as he kisses them—*ajak, nyelv, bőr, mellkas*—words all sounding as if they were unearthed from the steppes or blown in on the wind. Maybe because this is the first time anybody has fucked me since my ex-boyfriend. Maybe because it has been so long since I have let somebody touch me, rather than me just touching them. Maybe because I gave up control of my body and let another person play it for my pleasure, like the graduate student rimming me unexpectedly years ago. The spell lasts all night, and we are tangled together in my bed when Travis arrives the next morning. We wake to hear him in the kitchen, putting last night's dirty dishes into the dishwasher.

9

PARTIALLY TO KEEP my work life and my personal life as delineated as possible in an age where cell phones, instant messaging, and email act to corrupt our free time with work, partially to protect myself as a professor at a public institution with friends who send me pornographic emails and links to Web pages I would prefer not to access over the university computer system, I keep two separate email accounts. During the workday I check my school account constantly. My personal account, I often don't look at until evening. I am also old-fashioned when it comes to my cell phone: the ringer is always off during meetings, lectures, and my office hours. I demand the same from my students. So it is far into the afternoon when I check my voicemail and listen to the message from Lucinda asking if I've read my email yet. She makes some reference to an email I wrote attacking Ron, an email which, apparently, has all our friends riled up. I think she says something about me sending it to everybody. I log on to my personal account and find fifty-two messages in my inbox since last night. It takes me a while to sort through them, before I can make sense of it all.

Everything is due to a message from Pickle to me and cc'd to CJ and Allan.

From: Pickle
Date: Wednesday, March 3, 2004 5:17 AM
To: Damon
Cc: Allan, CJ
Subject: RE: Mongolian Rug

I just got back to town from the camel festival in the Gobi. I had to email you boys about this crazy coincidence. Before I get to the coincidence, let me say the camel races were amazing. Camels running look like those imperial walker things from The Empire Strikes Back. They were all awkward and unstable looking. The races are on this great plain, and people gather from all over to cheer on the riders from their village. And yes, Damon, there was plenty of fermented mare's milk. My favorite! I'm starting a chain of airag stores when I get back to WeHo. Fermented mare's milk will be the new boba!

Here is the crazy part. Remember that go-go boy from Mickey's you messed around with, CJ? That total drag-queen chaser? Remember how you fucked around on my couch and I was so jealous the next day because I'd been into him forever? The one that did the whole Polynesian tribal go-go routine with the spear and the wreaths around his head and wrists? I TOTALLY RAN INTO HIM AT THE CAMEL RACES!!!!!!

Yes, he also joined the Peace Corps. Said he had to get away from the stress of being a go-go boy and reconnect with what is real. He knew it was time to give up the business when he fell off a float he was dancing on in the Pride parade and broke his neck—he just couldn't figure out how to incorporate the neck brace into his go-go routine. He is stationed in Kazakhstan and was making his first trip out of the country!

Needless to say, he's relaxed his x-dressing requirements since being in the corps and made a detour to my yurt before heading back to Kazakhstan. He was all worried he was going to be celibate for the two years of his Peace Corps assignment. He's coming to see me in July during Naadam (the big national festival—tons of horse races and wrestling), but he did hint at bringing a burka for me to wear. Oh well. Maybe we'll introduce circuit parties to Central Asia.

Kisses,

Pickle

That wasn't the message that caused the uproar. The problem is that Pickle was responding to one of my messages from weeks ago, and he didn't erase my original message from below his. So the email continues:

-----Original Message------
From: Damon
Sent: Sunday, January 18, 2004 9:45 PM
To: Pickle
Subject: Mongolian Rug
Attach: RonAndAllanAndRug.JPG (150 KB) RugInFrontroom. JPG (150 KB) EveybodyByFire.JPG (150 KB) JohnnyDancingInKitchen.JPG (150 KB)

Pickle,
Such a vivid description of fermented mare's milk in your last

email. I could almost taste the salty tanginess in my mouth. Thanks!

I've attached photographs from the party. Ron and Allan were certainly moved by the rug you sent over for them. You can see from these pictures all the work they've done to fix up the house. The hot guy you don't recognize is Travis's man. If you're only going to go gay once a decade you might as well make it count, right?

I'm still having trouble adjusting to Ron and Allan's marriage thing. It is great for them to want to settle down, but couldn't Allan have done a better job choosing a partner? I mean, we all put up with Ron, but it is becoming more and more difficult. He seems to think people actually like him rather than just tolerate him for Allan's sake. How long can we be expected to endure his loathsome assholeishness?

Anyway, tell me all about the camel races when you get back.

Damon

Allan must have read his emails when he got into his office at the accounting firm and was quick to respond to my attack on Ron. Allan decided to send his response not only to me and CJ and Pickle, but to Lucinda, Travis, Seth, and Johnny as well. Ron is cc'd, of course. Allan goes on to include all these people who are not even a part of our core group of friends: Nathan, Hemp Guy (who Ron had tried to set me up with at the party), Denise, Russ, the guy who cuts both my hair and Allan's hair and who I've never hung out with socially, a few acquaintances whom I haven't spoken with in about a year (who I needed to get caught up with anyway), my ex-boyfriend,

Allan's chiropractor, a few members of the faculty here, and about a dozen other people whom I don't even recognize. The email reads:

From: Allan
Date: Wednesday, March 3, 2004 7:35 AM
To: the whole known world
Subject: RE: RE: Mongolian Rug

I am sick, and I am disappointed with all of you over your egregious treatment of Ron. Where do you all (most specifically, Damon) get your superior attitudes that make you think you can treat Ron so dismissively? What gives you the right to send emails over the oceans concerning the private affairs of my partner and me?

I have been reading this book, *Empowering Pride: Nurturing the Spirit of the Modern Gay Man* by Shaman John Ph.D., MFT, which I suggest you all pick up. This episode could be one of the case studies from the book, illustrating how internalized homophobia can jeopardize your happiness and the happiness of those around you. We need to learn how to be adults. There is a lot you could learn from this book, Damon.

Lucinda was the first to respond to Allan, again including everyone from Allan's message.

From: Lucinda
Date: Wednesday, March 3, 2004 8:07 AM
To: Everybody
Subject: RE: RE: RE: Mongolian Rug

Allan,

I'm not sure why I, my husband, all my friends and acquaintances (you even sent this to my mom!) got included on your response. I figure, however, that being included gives me the right to voice my opinion.

While I support your and Ron's relationship…well, come on…no matter how much you love Ron you can't be blind to how annoying he can be. Blowing off steam helps us to deal with him, and I'm sure that was all Damon was doing. And for even a moment do you really think internalized homophobia is *Damon's* problem?

Love you,

Lucinda

From:	CJ
Date:	Wednesday, March 3, 2004 8:42 AM
To:	Everybody
Subject:	RE: RE: RE: Mongolian Rug

Howdy everybody from Mexico! We've been up filming since dawn. All the boys have their makeup on, so I've got some time to chime in with my own grievances.

First, the rug is wondrous, but why didn't Damon attach a photo of Johnny and my present, too? The glass dino was exquisite! ;-)

Second, you guys have no shame emailing my boyfriend with tales of my fling with a go-go boy! Speaking of whom…did you take any photos of him, Pickle, before or during your camel-race hookup? Just to confirm he's the same guy, of course. Purely journalistic reasons.

Finally, you all need to check in concerning your costumes for Drag Strip next month. We're all going to finally make it to the club this month. OK, bitches? I've only heard from about half my entourage. Get your wigs ready! You're invited too, Lucinda's mom.

Cheers

From: Ron
Date: Wednesday, March 3, 2004 8:55 AM
To: Everybody
Subject: RE: RE: RE: Mongolian Rug

A pox on all of you for your frigidity! DO NOT THINK I WILL BE SILENCED. Rid me of your sickness! Rid me of your insanity!

From: Allan
Date: Wednesday, March 3, 2004 8:58 AM
To: Everybody
Subject: RE: RE: RE: RE: Mongolian Rug

Lucinda! I'm shocked to hear such homophobic trash from you as well. Since you enjoy full marriage rights from the state, it is obvious you can not relate to my plight.

After that message, the messages between Lucinda and Allan go back and forth, intensifying in vitriol, for the rest of the morning and into the early afternoon. Late in the morning Nathan even chimes in:

From: Nathan
Date: Wednesday, March 3, 2004 11:26 AM
To: Everybody
Subject: RE: RE: RE: RE: Mongolian Rug

Thanks for including me in your email exchange even though I've only met many of you once!

Could we get back to the whole drag-queen-chasing-go-go-boy thread? CJ: did you find a lot of these guys? Were they good in bed? I agree that photos would be useful.

Nathan also sent a message to just me:

From: Nathan
Date: Wednesday, March 3, 2004 11:28 AM
To: Damon
Subject: Travis's Man?

Thanks for calling me out as the go-to-guy for once in a decade gay experiences. This would probably be awkward if we weren't now fucking. Can't wait to get you alone tonight!

Lucinda's most recent email calls for a de-escalation of sorts:

From: Lucinda
Date: Wednesday, March 3, 2004 2:37 PM
To: Everybody
Subject: RE: RE: RE: RE: RE: RE: RE: RE: RE: Mongolian Rug

Allan, obviously this subject still needs more discussion, but at least I think it is time we stop emailing so many people about it. You made your point about the large spectrum of people who have negative feelings about Ron, although I still take exception with your characterization of it as a "vast conspiracy." Either way, let's limit further emails to just the handful of people central to the issue—or better yet—just meet to talk about this in person.

After finishing Lucinda's message, written less than ten minutes ago, I first walk down the hall to find the two colleagues that made the email list. They are the other faculty members I occasionally see socially outside of the university, and I suspect Allan got their addresses from Evites I had sent for get-togethers at my condo. Anyway, we have a good laugh about it, and I apologize for their inboxes getting flooded with such junk. Last year, one faculty member had a screaming match in the middle of the faculty hallway with his ex-wife who is department head in a liberal arts department across campus, so this incident is comparably tame.

I give Lucinda a call next, expecting her to be concerned and serious. Instead, she is already giggling when she picks up the phone.

"What a mess you have made," she says. "Why haven't you jumped into the fray?"

I explain that I just finished reading the emails and have another appointment at 3:00. "I'll think about it carefully and send something out tonight."

"Damon, everything you said was true and probably needed to be expressed. Well, up to the point where you brought up 'his loathsome assholeishness.' I think that was the point where you jumped right over the line from saying the things that need to be said to just being nasty. Where did you even come up with that phrase, loathsome assholeishness?"

Soon after Allan had gotten his HIV diagnosis, he and my ex-boyfriend had started going dancing every Tuesday and Thursday at this gay country bar in Studio City, Oil Can Harry's. This was before I got tenure, so I was working late all the time. I was happy my ex-boyfriend was getting out, but I teased him a little for going line-dancing. I think it was Johnny who had originally suggested the place to Allan. Through his volunteer work Johnny knew some twelve-steppers who went there because it was a welcoming scene and not as alcohol-centric as West Hollywood.

There were always classes between 7:30 and 9:00 to help the new people learn the dances. Their first night at the club Allan came right from work and still wore a tie and a button shirt; my ex-boyfriend wore tennis shoes ill-suited to dancing. They arrived fifteen minutes before the classes were to start, and the place was nearly empty. A little nervous, they ordered drinks from the bartender. Allan loosened his tie. His clothes would have looked less out of place in nearly any LA bar other than this one; silk ties and pressed shirts were an odd contrast with the cowhides and old rifles adorning the walls. A huge papier-mâché cowboy hat with a band of Christmas tree lights on the brim hung above the dance floor.

The lessons were divided into two parts: first one of the partner dances such as the waltz, the two-step, or the western swing, followed by instruction on two different line dances. The partner dances were easier to pick up, so only eight people were there when class began. The instructor was assisted by a younger, quiet lady whom all the boys would marvel at when she effortlessly two-stepped around the floor with her partner.

The dance that night was the waltz. Even with rubber-soled shoes that did not glide on the wood floor, my ex, nimble on his feet and no stranger to dancing, was able to carry Allan through the lesson easily. Allan had not done enough formal dancing to be thrown by starting with his right foot rather than his left or by holding my ex-boyfriend's left hand in his right, and if they didn't quite float through the two practice songs (old Patsy Cline followed by "My Favorite Things" with pedal steel), they didn't stumble or step on each other's feet either.

The line-dancing instruction, however, was different. The bar had filled by then and Allan and my ex-boyfriend had followed the instructor's suggestion and made their way to the front row, right before the stage, where she encouraged all the beginners to stand so she could watch over them and they could best see her and her assistants on the stage. The instructor's assistant from the waltz stood on her left, graceful as ever, and a young man with a crew cut stood on her right. Crew-Cut Guy wore his gingham shirt tucked into his jeans and rolled far up his forearms.

As much as he watched the people on the stage or my ex-boyfriend beside him, Allan could not pick up the line dances. He felt particularly angry with the instructor. Not that the woman teaching the class humiliated Allan or made fun of him for his inability to pick up the moves, not that she even singled him out and explained the footwork to him slowly as one might to a dim child, not that she even made disappointed frowns in his direction, she simply never

142

praised him the way she did other new students. When she said to my ex-boyfriend, "Great, but lead with your hips a little more on the third turn," Allan felt the sting of not winning an authority figure's recognition.

Allan kept finding himself facing north when the whole array of people on the floor faced south. He would miscount steps and crash into my ex-boyfriend, who would give him a supportive smile, or he would crash into the short, serious man on his other side, who would give him a glare and a huff. It got so bad that he fled the dance floor in frustration.

My ex was already finding his country groove and thinking about shopping for boots. He felt twin disappointments: both that his well-intentioned outing did not yield a night of harmless distraction for his friend, and that Allan's frustration meant they would probably not be coming back here on Thursday night. He decided to let Allan sulk on his own for a while and finish learning the dance.

When the woman finished her instructions, she had the crowd applaud her assistants, the DJ, the guy taking money at the door, and the men working the bar. She left the stage along with her assistants and had the DJ put on two songs so that the crowd could practice the line dance they had learned. My ex ran through both these practices and remembered all the moves. He only messed up the timing of one turn but looked at his neighbor's feet and fell right in step. When the people taking the lesson broke up and the real dancing was to being for the night, he went to look for Allan. He found him in the far corner of the club with the crew-cut guy who had been one of the assistants on the stage.

They were not socializing; Crew-Cut Guy was standing beside Allan, teaching him the steps to the first line dance. The pace was slower, with more encouragement than Allan received in the group lesson. When he saw what was going on, my ex stopped; he leaned against the wall and watched the two of them from a little ways off. Allan made a mistake, and Crew-Cut Guy punched him (but not too hard) in the shoulder. Allan's eyes sparkled with the punch. If he couldn't gain the carrot, he should at least feel the snap of the stick.

Like in any wild population, environmental pressures weed out men, catering to those who show a propensity for certain behaviors and punishing those who insist on others. When we were all running around in hides, spearing wildebeest and picking berries, was there any adaptive advantage for those OCD cavemen who would insist on lining up all the rocks in the cave in perfect rows or who had to make sure that the twigs in the kindling crossed each other at perfect ninety–degree angles? They were probably the first ones eaten by dire wolves. Enough survived, however, for their descendants to flourish in the modern world. What traits could better ensure one's survival in the era of police states, Martha Stewart-inspired housewifery, and cubicled bean counters than obsessive-compulsive predilections and blind subservience to authority?

My ex-boyfriend watched Allan's progress under Crew-Cut Guy's tutelage. He soon felt like a voyeur, so he watched the

144

crowd dancing instead. He watched a man in a dark cowboy hat with a large, silver belt buckle. The man knew all the moves of the line dances, and his two-stepping included footwork and turns my ex-boyfriend couldn't even parse, much less hope to reproduce. The song ended, and everyone looked for new partners.

Considering the man's skills, my ex-boyfriend hesitated when the man came up to him and asked him to be his partner. He was sure he could do the basic two-step footwork, but not those elaborate turns and twirls. The man in the dark hat understood his apprehension.

"I'll take it easy on you," he said with a goofy, lop-sided grin.

The grin won my ex over. He reassured himself that his feet just needed to keep the beat of the dance, and the rest of him needed to consign itself to the lead of the dark-hated man. After the first few seconds in the man's arms, he lost sense of his position in the room, lost track of all the other couples, and just trusted the man to steer him around the dance floor. Nothing existed apart from the endless looping of the fast-fast-slow-slow rhythm of the two-step and the man's grip on him, a grip through which the man transmitted subtle cues, slight pulls and pushes that dictated all his moves. My ex-boyfriend submitted his whole volition to the other and realized the man had him performing twirls he didn't know how to do. He ricocheted around like a molecule of a simple fluid. For the few minutes of the dance, my ex-boyfriend was liberated from all the responsibility and untidy decisions in his life. Maybe he had already started thinking of moving to Boston. The music ended. The guy shook his hand, thanked him for the dance, and went to find another partner. Everyone in the club seemed to dance with everybody else; everyone rotated partners after every song.

The club had grown too crowded for Allan and Crew-Cut Guy to continue their lesson, so they were just standing and talking. Allan saw my ex-boyfriend and motioned him over.

My ex-boyfriend was naturally affable: he could talk genially with someone he just met in a bar without being flirtatious. He walked over to Allan and Crew-Cut Guy and fell into conversation with them.

"You must be a dancer," said Crew-Cut Guy immediately. "When I'm up there helping with the classes, I can always spot the other dancers in the crowd."

"Not really a dancer," said my ex-boyfriend. "You're going to laugh; it's the gayest thing ever."

"I knew it, you're a Cirque du Soleil acrobat," said Crew-Cut Guy excitedly. "You have the calves of an acrobat."

Crew-Cut Guy squatted on the floor and gripped my ex-boyfriend's left calf to feel the muscle. My ex kept his composure while having his leg felt up by the stranger.

"Wow, you don't have any boundaries, do you?" said my ex. "What was your name?"

"Ron," he said, not yet getting up off the floor.

"Well, Ron, what I was going to say is that I was really into cheerleading when I was in high school and college, so I pick up

146

choreography fairly fast. I think cheerleading is probably gayer than acrobatics, don't you think? I even coached cheerleading for a while after college, but then I moved to Santa Barbara and fell out of the loop. Coaching cheerleading is one of those things that is all about connections. Now I just jerk caffeine at Starbucks, and the only cheering I do is constant encouragement of my boyfriend. Ron, I think you need to stand up now."

"What did you say your name was?" said Ron, popping up.

"Felix," said my ex-boyfriend.

"You totally need to be careful how much caffeine you take in, Felix. Did you know you can absorb it through your skin at work? I read that it causes your hair to fall out. I mean, your hair looks good, but you do have some widow's peaks, so be careful."

With the extra instruction from Ron, Allan was happy to go back to the club with Felix on Thursday. He and Felix kept returning, learning all the dances and becoming regulars. Within a month Felix had shirts with mother-of-pearl buttons.

By the time Ron and Allan went on their first date a few weeks later, Allan had realized his diagnosis was not a death sentence; rather, it was a mandate that his body was no longer an object to be taken for granted, but a thing to be assiduously managed. Even with the immediate threat of death denuded, the diagnosis and shock waves emanating from it into every aspect of his life (not just his health came into consideration, but the loyalty of his friends, the degree to which he should disclose his status in the workplace, his very reckoning of the future) made his HIV status something he thought about constantly, researched constantly. It was so much on his mind that it was nearly the first thing he said to Ron on that first date, right between what he wanted Ron to order for him at the espresso bar (double non-fat mocha, no whip) and where he wanted to sit (on the patio, considering the warmth of the summer evening).

Ron had several HIV-positive friends and was unperturbed by his date's revelation. One date turned into half a dozen; mostly they attended plays and performance pieces in which Ron's friends appeared, followed by late, intimate dinners in which they debated the merits of the show they had just seen and shared stories of everything from their childhoods to their favorite parts of the city to the people they hated at work. While the emotional confidences between the two men deepened, their physical relationship did not progress beyond light kissing.

Ron understood the thrill of flirtation and seduction, the rush of being lust's object, the pain of being rebuffed, the sting of jealousy. But truth be told, when it came to the physical act of lovemaking itself—his penis, the other guy's penis, placing one or the other into the body of the partner—he was largely ambivalent. After six dates, however, he and Allan were in some sort of relationship—whether it ultimately settled on casual or committed, transient or enduring—and propriety dictated that someone should be ejaculating somewhere by now. Ron's pride, if not his reptile brain, demanded it.

So, at the end of date six, as Allan was driving him home from another night at the theater, Ron asked bluntly what was going on between them. Why weren't they having sex?

For Allan, the exhilaration of those rare moments in which he completely transcended his nature fueled him, on a subconscious level, to create difficult, impossible situations in his life, just for the sake of being able to conquer them. In other words, he created problems so he could overcome them, but overcome them in a manner he thought beyond his ability, which necessitated creating problems he didn't think he was capable of overcoming in the first place. And many times, this transcending himself amounted to a moment of complete and painful clarity: being honest with himself and being able, at least momentarily, to articulate that honesty.

This was such a moment in Allan's life. In the simple act of responding to Ron's question, he could erase years of secrets, denial, and veiled impulses he hardly understood.

"I need to be dominated," he said. "I need to be torn screaming from my impulse to control everything and forced to surrender to another person to be happy, especially sexually. I need to transgress and be punished. Occasionally, I need to be beaten. I was embarrassed to share that with you. It is easier with strangers." The moment he finished speaking these words, he realized he may never again be able to articulate his feelings so accurately. Some things in life, however, only need to be done correctly once, and Allan had chosen to speak these words to the one person to whom they would matter.

Although often dismissed as a fool, Ron could do the calculations in his head. Here was a guy—attractive enough, fun enough to be around, hard working, good salary, thinking of buying

149

a house, dependable—and the cost of this was some bondage, whipping, and his assuming the role of a dominant top. He had dabbled in leather before, and as for playing the master—was he not a student of the theater? Was he not a thespian?

It seemed like a fair deal to Ron, and he considered this car ride his audition. He waited until Allan was driving nearly eighty miles per hour down the 134. Ron leaned over and abruptly cinched Allan's lap belt so that both it and the shoulder strap tightened against Allan.

"What the fuck are you doing?" screamed Allan at his date's unexpected behavior.

"Shut the fuck up," Ron yelled back. The car careened around the carpool lane. "Concentrate on the fucking road or you'll get both of us killed, for fuck's sake."

As Ron started to unzip Allan's fly, Allan attempted to push Ron away with his right arm. Allan's control of the car was already compromised, however. He found he had to keep both hands on the steering wheel to keep from colliding with the center divider. He thought about kneeing Ron in the head, but he realized his right foot was effectively bound to the gas pedal.

Despite Allan's vehement protests, Ron found him erect when he worked his way into his pants. Ron teased Allan's hard-on out of the folds of his underwear and buried it in his mouth. Due to the car's cramped quarters, Ron decided to keep his hands out of the way. A hands-free blowjob would be appropriate: focus on sucking and depth in the mouth, forget about tandem sucking of the head and manual stroking of the shaft. Ron was a man who liked to concentrate on form while blowing another man, so he found Allan's screaming a distraction. Ron sat up.

"We need to jam something in that mouth of yours to shut you up," he said. He glanced around the car; it was immaculate. Ron hastily removed his left shoe and sock and forced the balled-up sock into Allan's mouth, fighting his way past his clenched teeth. Admiring his own ingenuity with the sock, Ron was grateful for all the improv classes he had attended.

Between the constraints of the seatbelt, Ron's head wedged between his stomach and the steering wheel, the sock in his mouth, and the focus required to navigate down the freeway with all these distractions, Allan was having the most fulfilling date of his life. By the time they reached Ron's apartment in Glendale, the front of Allan's pants was slathered in semen, and the bond between the two men was cemented.

Even though Felix considered Allan his best friend, he did not understand Allan's infatuation with Ron. Like the rest of us, he found Ron difficult. However, Felix continued going with Allan to Oil Can Harry's twice a week, where they would meet up with Ron after he helped with the classes. More correctly, Allan would meet up with Ron, and Felix would spend the rest of the night dancing away from them.

As I am driving home from work, I think about back then, and how inconceivable it would have been for me that within a couple of years Felix and I would be living on opposite sides of the continent, never speaking, and Allan and Ron would be planning a commitment ceremony.

Before I even unlock my condo door, I can hear Nathan playing his viola inside. I enter as quietly as possible. Travis is on the couch, listening. Nathan is seated on a chair from the dining-room table, placed in the middle of the room. I sit on an armchair and listen to the rest of the sonata.

Travis and I clap when Nathan finishes, and he puts his instrument away. Nathan is obviously pleased with our response. Beaming, he walks over and kisses me deeply.

"Not in front of the kid," I say.

"You are upset about all the turmoil you caused?" Nathan says.

"A little. I'll get online after dinner and get up to date on the messages. I should send out a response before I go to bed."

When I do finally log on, the first message is from Russ, responding to Lucinda's call to scale back the number of people receiving emails:

From: Russell
Date: Wednesday, March 3, 2004 3:17 PM
To: Everybody
Subject: RE: RE: RE: RE: RE: RE: RE: RE: RE: RE: Mongolian Rug

No, no, no! Please don't cut me from the distribution list. This is better than the current season of Survivor.

Russell

Otherwise, the pace of the emails did slow a little after Lucinda's plea for restraint.

From: Pickle
Date: Wednesday, March 3, 2004 6:19 PM
To: Everybody
Subject: RE: RE: RE: RE: RE: RE: RE: RE: RE: RE: Mongolian Rug

OMG, you guys, I can't believe I caused all this. Please don't think for a minute I did it on purpose, it was totally me being a bubblehead. But I think you all maybe need to chill out a bit. We are all going to stick together in the end, and I think Damon was just venting like Lucinda said. But seriously, everyone needs to peace out. This is all out of control.

I just got up and the sun is rising over Ulaanbaatar while it is setting on you guys. I can't believe I caused all this on the other side of the world.

From: CJ
Date: Wednesday, March 3, 2004 7:43 PM
To: Everybody
Subject: RE: RE: RE: RE: RE: RE: RE: RE: RE: RE: Mongolian Rug

We finished shooting for the day, so I'm back at the hotel freshening up. Just got on my wig and my sarong, and now Ms. CJ is going to unwind in the tropical evening with a mai tai on the hotel bar's veranda.

Cheers to Damon and Pickle! Just when our jokes about Seth and Lucinda's "what to do if you are having a heart attack"

Christmas card started to wane, someone else in the group steps up and does something outrageous we will be laughing about for months. "Loathsome assholeishness" can officially replace "raise your arms, grin, and repeat this simple sentence" as out favorite catchphrase. Bravo!

As for Nathan's questions: the brashness you have to ask me such things! Unbelievable! But since you asked….that particular go-go boy was really the beginning of the end of my days as a happy-go-lucky bachelorette. The go-go boy was hot (where are those pictures, Pickle?), and the sex was too perfect (nothing compared to you, Johnny, of course). The only thing extraordinary about the situation might have been that he was unusually young to be aware of and willing to act on his drag-queen kink. Usually, it is not until guys reach their 30s that they possess the confidence to pursue a sex partner in front of their peers that deviates from the accepted norm—that is to say, hot twinks. Anyway, with that go-go boy I felt like I crossed the line from fun, lusty hookups to something mechanical and practiced. I felt like I was having sex like a porn star: all technique and no heart. There is an age when sex is all excitement and discovery—the new gift we must learn to use, but to be an adult is to define sex in our lives. So yes, Nathan, sex with the go-go boys of this world was easy to find and quite amazing, but at some point it just made me a robot. I had to reach out on another level to bring me back and make it meaningful again.

But I digress! Now that Sex and the City is off the air, maybe we could develop these emails into a show for HBO called "Drama Bitches." Ha, ha, ha!!

From: Ron
Date: Wednesday, March 3, 2004 7:43 PM
To: Everybody
Subject: RE: RE: RE: RE: RE: RE: RE: RE: RE: RE: RE:

154

Mongolian Rug

Et tu Pickle? I can't believe even you are defending Damon.

Travis goes to bed early, explaining he's been getting up particularly early to work on some new sculptures. Nathan immediately tries to pull me into bed, but I insist I write my email first.

From: Damon
Date: Wednesday, March 3, 2004 9:15 PM
To: Everybody
Subject: RE: RE: RE: RE: RE: RE: RE: RE: RE: RE: RE: Mongolian Rug

I can't pretend that I don't feel the things I said about Ron, but I can not excuse the hurtful way in which they were communicated. For that I need to apologize. Also, I am sorry for all of you who have gotten dragged into this exchange despite being far removed from the conflict. Please do not blame Pickle for anything. He has said nothing derogatory about Ron; he was just acting as my sounding board. While I thank Lucinda for sticking up for me, this is nobody's fault but my own. Ron and Allan, please direct your anger at me alone.

Damon

10

Sunday afternoon Russ and I are having coffee outside the Peet's on Main in Santa Monica. He was away for his birthday—a trip to Australia for his older sister's wedding—and between our packed schedules and his jetlag, this is the first chance we've had to get together. I offered to treat him to dinner, but he wanted to drive out here for coffee instead. The Peet's is in a mini-mall designed by Frank Gehry, and Russ needed to photograph it for a school project.

I was skeptical about driving all this way for Gehry, since I am not a fan of his new concert hall. I'm sure the hall looks great from a helicopter or on a design table, but the way you experience it walking down Grand Avenue is only as walls of metal, cold and dead. Here at Edgemar, there is a consciousness about how buildings and people interact. The angular cement forms create unexpected corners of serenity; the buildings surround a courtyard that engenders public sociability in a city often bereft of it. Maybe being in Ocean Park suggests it to me, but the light hitting the pale tile and chain link makes me think of a Diebenkorn painting.

Russ is running around taking photographs. He stands on some steps, shooting pictures of the glass atrium atop one of the building's towers, when he shouts my name. I turn abruptly, and he takes a candid picture. He looks at the camera's display and laughs; I must have looked frazzled after being startled from my thoughts.

"OK," he says. "Now smile this time, so I get one without you looking goofy."

I oblige him. He finishes documenting the building and joins me back at the table. I ask Russ if he is dating anybody again, and he rolls his eyes. He says he is really bitter about men right now.

"What is this all about?" I ask.

He asks me if I have read this week's *SpunkyLA*, one of the city's free weekly LGBT newspapers. I tell him I haven't seen it.

"Good," says Russ. "Then I can start at the beginning."

Russ works a couple days a week at an independent bookstore in Los Feliz. A little over a month ago a guy came in and started browsing the magazines. He glanced at Russ a couple times and smiled when he caught Russ's eye. He brought some tabloids to the counter and started talking with Russ while Russ ran his credit card. The store was quiet. He and Russ continued flirting for a while, until the guy finally wrote down his address in West Hollywood and invited Russ over after work.

"The guy was very cute and seemed nice enough," says Russ,

"so I decided to take a chance and go over to his house. I was careful about everything—left his address with my roommates in case I ended up hacked to pieces in an alley. And the other clerk working that afternoon assured me that the guy had a good vibe. I should have known not to trust a man who goes into an independent bookstore and buys nothing but trashy tabloids."

"The guy already had his shirt off when he opened the door, emerging from a cloud of pot smoke," continues Russ. "He got me a glass of wine, and we sat on his couch. A little too loudly, he told me he was from New Hampshire. When I told him I was from Orange County, he started talking about Laguna Beach and how much he likes its gay scene because there aren't so many immigrants around."

"So you pretty much lost your shit," I say, anticipating Russ's response.

"Long story short, my wine ended up in his face and I was home in time to catch *The Daily Show*. That should have been it, just another random dumb guy you make fun of with your friends and never see again. Then, last week at four in the morning I was up with insomnia reading *SpunkyLA*."

Russ fishes around in his messenger bag and pulls out a newsprint clipping. Aryan Stoner Fuck, it turns out, is one of the columnists for *SpunkyLA*. Russ hands me the clipping to read:

Lush Life
By Waldo X

Can't shake this malaise that's befallen me since turning thirty. Decide the cure lies in eliciting love from a new stranger every day this week.

Monday, the bank teller. I was dismayed when my boutique bank was bought by a behemoth McFinancial Institution, and I was forced to begin standing in line with the masses. The Adonis of a teller who helps me goes a long way to restoring my customer loyalty—especially when he follows up with a house call for some deposits and withdrawals of a more private nature. Somehow believes he can stay overnight, but I inform him my bedroom has fewer perks than his bank. I tell him to take a number and send him to the back of the line.

Sipping Grey Goose on the East/West patio Tuesday night, an inebriated ingénue asks for a cigarette. He seems to have lost track of his friends but does find his way into my bed. The mood is almost ruined by the drag queen next door practicing her Beyoncé routine, but I throw a few ice cubes over the fence to quiet her down.

Wednesday, the nerdy hottie at Skylight Books. I am shwing a client a house in Los Feliz and I end up early for my appointment when traffic is unexpectedly light. Stop in to rub elbows with the literati since I have time to kill. The cashier—maybe his name was Russell—takes little more than a wink and my card to convince him to show up at my house after his shift. The bookish ones really are wildcats in bed. The darling— is he even old enough to drink?—wonders if we could go on a "date" sometime. As I'm showing him the door, I explain to him how déclassé it is to date those in the service sector.

Thursday, I opt for the stud always in a tie and flamenco shoes at the gay gym.

Friday, my handyman. I'm not one for celebrity crushes—but I make an exception for the stunning carpenter on Refurbishing Rooms. (I don't care what they say—he is such a homo, and I've heard he lives here in LA.) Stopping by a house I'm flipping, my handyman is hanging new French doors. Figure this is as close as I'll get to my fantasy carpenter for now. Tell handyman to put down the doors and go to work on me.

Sitting on my front porch Saturday, cock my head and flash my irresistible smile at a natty gent walking his dog. Poochie gets to wait in the backyard, leash tied to my patio table.

Open house on Sunday makes it almost too easy—parade of moneyed homos all afternoon—but I deserve it easy after my week-long pursuit of love. I think I might have to settle for a quickie in the pantry with one domestic partner while the other domestic partner is casing the master bath, but decide to double down and hit up a hot pair for a three-way. Faster than you can say "subprime," I get a pair of horny homo house-hunters to retire with me to the pool house. When the market's this hot, I don't really need to work at selling the house anyway.

"What a fucking glib prick," I say. "Look, nobody pays any attention to those columns anyway. Isn't this one run right next to the nonsensical one from the gay shaman guy?"

"Yes, and as a side note, you would be appalled by the crap that Shaman John Ph.D., MFT, said in the same issue. He wrote a column demanding older gays act as better role models and mentors within the community—which is great—but he introduced the

160

article by bragging about how he can't multiply by numbers greater than seven and trying to pass off his ignorance as an act of civil disobedience."

"That's great," I say sarcastically. "I spend my weeks trying to get my students to care about real science, and Dr. Drum Circle is reveling in his inability to perform basic arithmetic."

"Anyway, back to my problems. Did Aryan Stoner Fuck have to not only make up those lies but include my name and workplace in his article? I've been having to explain this at work and at school. It is degrading."

"Obviously, the guy is not well. Sex is nothing more than a way to mask his own insecurities. Especially, it seems, if that sex involves humiliating others."

"It just sucks," moans Russ. "I am so sick of stupid men."

I shiver with a sudden chill and feel terribly embarrassed. "Russ," I ask, "you never felt like this with me, did you? I'm not that guy, am I?"

"Certainly not. Did you print lies about me in the paper?"

"I guess not."

"You never treated me disrespectfully before or after our fling. I totally didn't make any connection between that creep and you. Look, you're still single, right?"

I pause for a moment in indecision.

"Well," I say, "I guess not. I'm sort of seeing somebody. It is complicated."

"What?" says Russ. The look on his face is difficult to read.

I ask him if he remembers Nathan from the long email war a few weeks back.

"You're seeing him? Did he and Travis break up?" asks Russ.

"No," I say.

"You are messing around with your best friend's guy behind his back?" Russ seems agitated that he would even have to ask such a question.

"No. None of that. Travis knows, and they are still together."

"It is a three-way relationship?"

"Yes. I suppose. Except I'm not sleeping with Travis, but really Nathan and Travis don't sleep together either. But they still spend a lot of time together like they are dating. Except, with all this going on, I guess Travis and I are spending more time than usual together, too."

"So this has been going on for some time."

"Maybe a month or so."

"Does anybody else know?"

"You're the second person I've told. Lucida was the first."

"How did that go?" asks Russ

I tell him it went far worse than I had imagined.

Travis had been upset with me for being secretive about my affair with Nathan. I had told none of our friends and asked Travis to remain silent about it, too. Travis repeatedly told me that one only keeps secrets about things that, on some level, one is ashamed of. I could justify the secrecy for a short time, arguing that Nathan and I had only messed around once or twice. The whole thing, most probably, would run its course as quickly as it had begun, and there was no sense inviting problems about something so fleeting. Soon it became undeniable that sex with Nathan had become a fixture in my life, and I decided to listen to Travis as my conscience and be open with our friends. He was especially eager that I talk to Lucinda.

I told Lucinda in person, over lunch at her house, while Seth was out on a long training ride. After a few moments of disbelief, she made me clarify all that I had told her and reaffirm that Nathan and I were having sex with Travis's full consent, while Nathan and Travis were still seeing one another. Then she fell into a few more minutes of disbelief, followed by complete discomfort on both our parts. Finally, she lit into me with everything she could think of that was wrong with what I was doing. The main points of her argument included (but were not limited to) the following:

1. Travis's sexuality was fragile and damaged at best. As one of his oldest and closest friends, how could I be oblivious to this? Certainly my involvement in Travis's romantic life put Travis and my friendship in jeopardy.

2. Since Nathan lives in Budapest, our tryst was necessarily transient. Why would I risk Travis's friendship over a man with an expiration date anyway?

3. And removing the issue of Travis from consideration, granted, Nathan was handsome and charming, but wasn't I old enough and smart enough to know better when it came to guys like that? Did I really think Nathan was capable of a real relationship?

4. And even if I am to be given some slack because this was

my first attempt at dating after a painful separation and the requisite fucking around: well, *really*, shouldn't I know better?

5. And if I were indeed ready to attempt a real relationship again: wasn't diddling away my time with Nathan distracting me from more appropriate partners?

As a retort, I told her that I was looking for neither her permission nor her advice, told her to stop being so codependent, and stormed out of her house. Travis, at least, was relieved that he could return to living a life of complete honesty.

Russ's response is more muted than Lucinda's; he doesn't seem to know what to say about the three-way relationship.

"If all three of our needs are being met," I say to break the silence, "what is wrong with lighting out for the territories? What is wrong with exploring new forms? Who cares if we aren't following the usual monogamous-couple model?"

"Nothing, I guess," he accedes. Then he changes the subject. "I burned a copy of that Sufjan Stevens album I was telling you about. Let me give it to you before I forget."

He goes into his messenger bag again, this time taking out a CD in a plain jewel case and sliding it across the table to me. We talk about albums and movies for quite a while until we begin our drive home.

11

WHEN CJ MOVED INTO JOHNNY'S HOUSE, he turned it into a giant cabinet of wonders. Johnny was indifferent to interior decorating. He let CJ throw away the aging couches and bureaus that had been bought at garage sales, let CJ rip out the stained beige carpets, and let CJ tear down the venetian blinds that hid the wall of windows in the living room. Behind those venetian blinds was one of the finest views from the Silver Lake hills.

CJ filled the cleansed house with items from his travels around the globe with *Surf/Trek*. I've been to their house so many times that I forget how overwhelming it is. Nathan's mouth, however, falls open when we walk in the front door. The house is like a cross between the Natural History Museum and your grandfather's attic. Shelves are lined with geodes, the lacquered exoskeletons of horseshoe crabs, chambered nautiluses, dried fruit and pods from exotic vines, and starfish the size of platters. Johnny has allowed the trees on the slope below to grow up and into the windows. On the walls hang large pieces of driftwood; epiphytes such as orchids and bromeliads are planted in the wood's crooks and hollows. Between these hanging gardens are ceremonial masks from seemingly every island culture on the planet. Most of the lights hanging from the ceiling are inside glass polyhedra that are shaped like stars. Every end table and coffee table is littered with fossilized trilobites and shark teeth, ships in bottles, and handmade gongs, bells, and drums.

CJ and Johnny have a soft heart for animals as well. In the center of the room is a play area for their macaw, Mateo, formed from long bamboo poles and a giant metal model of the solar system. There are two saltwater aquariums—one in which clown fish play among sea anemones, one in which sea horses grip a fan coral with their tails and cowfish hover like alien landing craft. A third fish tank was converted into a terrarium to house tree frogs.

The plan was for all of us to gather at CJ and Johnny's house to have dinner and get ready for Drag Strip, but when Nathan and I arrive, Johnny is the only one there. CJ had been at the club, helping with the decorations, when a call came in that one of the ladies scheduled to perform had suffered an accident and would be unable to participate in the show. For the first time ever, CJ was invited to do one of his routines. It was a big honor. He is staying at the club longer than expected to practice on the stage but will be along for dinner in about an hour.

Nathan starts wandering around the living room, playing some of the percussion instruments and watching the clown fish burry themselves in their anemones.

I tell Johnny that Travis is going to be late too. He is deep into working on one of his sculptures and does not want to stop for a few more hours. Denise, his ex-girlfriend, is going to pick him up and meet us at the club.

"Allan and Ron will also meet us at the club, if they show up at all," says Johnny. "My gosh, Allan is still pissed at you about that email. He didn't want to have dinner with us when he heard you were going to be here. You both need to chill out tonight and just be cool again."

Johnny is not interested in dwelling on the email incident. "It is super nice up on the sundeck," says Johnny. "Why don't you guys go up there? I'll get us some pomegranate juice and be right up."

Nathan follows me up a set of stairs to the roof where CJ and Johnny have a patio. Since the last time I was there, they built a little arbor for shade in one corner, filled it with potted plants, and draped netting around it to form an aviary. Finches flutter, and a flock of tiny quail dart about on the ground.

"This place is insane," says Nathan.

Johnny comes up the stairs with a tray of drinks and chips. He puts it down and joins us next to the aviary.

"I love this, especially listening to the finches when I have my coffee in the mornings. CJ and I are adding a fountain next, to give the birdies more water. I'm a little afraid, though; this will be ground zero when avian flu hits Los Angeles."

Johnny beckons Nathan and me to sit in the two lawn chairs,

and he lies on the chaise lounge.

"I got a bunch of this juice at Sam's Club last week. It is supposed to be so purifying. Did you know I quit smoking two weeks ago?"

This is indeed news to me. Johnny has smoked heavily since I have known him and has shown no signs of letting up before this.

"I started training for the AIDS marathon, and I just can't hang with the group when my lungs are like this," he explains.

"Are you still feeling the withdrawals?" asks Nathan.

"Not so much. Except I know I'll smoke after having a few drinks tonight. That seems inevitable. I've been scuba diving again, too. Another reason to act kindly to my lungs. I used to go a lot, years ago, when I ran away to San Diego to become a bartender. You would not believe the amount of sea creatures out there, just a little ways off the beach. You would think we have killed and poisoned everything, but life grabs hold wherever it can; it is relentless. Anything that is able to survive is out there growing and mating and reproducing. The guys I volunteer with at that youth cycling program in Santa Monica like to go diving on Catalina. So I've been going with them now and then. They free dive, too—but I'm not ready for that. You swim down deep without any tanks, just holding your breath. The blue surrounds you. Plus, because you have no tanks and regulators, you make no mechanical noises. You don't scare away any animals. Mantas glide right past you; even whales swim over and check you out."

Johnny now starts to free associate: "Did you two ever think about how the hugest adult giant squid was once small enough to swim around in your coffee cup? Or those woolly mammoths they dig up in the arctic, what about those? And maybe if we just plant a lot of bamboo we could have pandas in the Sierras."

Johnny takes a long gulp of pomegranate juice, puts it down, and stretches out on the lounge. "You two are dating now—or something like that—that's what the talk is. Right?"

"Yes," I say, "Nathan and Travis and I."

"I totally didn't bring it up to judge," he says. "I didn't want it to be the elephant in the room. Please don't think it is gossiping. Between the email barrage and your fight with Lucinda, it is a little hard not to talk about it."

"I figured everyone would know everything after the argument with Lucinda," I say.

Johnny's attention doesn't focus on one subject for long. He quickly turns to a new topic: "CJ gave me that CD of your quartet, Nate. Classical music isn't really my thing, but I've gotten into listening to it."

"Thanks, man," says Nathan. "It is always great to hear that from new listeners. Did you say you used to bartend?"

"I was like twenty-three. It was fun at the time. I got to do a lot of things I wouldn't have otherwise had a chance to try."

"I bet you did," says Nathan with a naughty smile.

"Yah, I bet it is like that for you, traveling around as a professional musician."

They both chuckle like they're part of the same club. I feel like I am in a fucking frat house. It goes on like this for another half hour, the two of them recounting their adventures. I occasionally get up to watch the birds in the aviary. Finally, CJ gets home.

We hear CJ pull into the driveway, and Johnny yells down to him to join us on the sundeck. I can hear his heels clicking on the stairs long before he appears. Besides the stilettos, he is wearing unremarkable grey sweat pants and a white T-shirt. He doesn't have on a wig or makeup. The incongruity of the outfit must register on my face because he quickly explains he is trying to break in the new shoes for tonight. He had to practice his routine in them, he explains. "I never mix boy and girl stuff like this. I hate it. Trust me, tonight I'll look like a trollop in animal pelts."

"I already broached the whole three-way-relationship thing with them," says Johnny to CJ, "so it isn't awkward or anything."

"Good boy," says CJ, "then I don't need to do it myself. Are you guys ready for some dinner? Sorry the only hors d'oeuvres my man can serve are generic corn chips."

For Johnny, dining out means one thing: getting ripped off. Everywhere charges too much. You are a chump unless you go to Costco, buy in bulk, and prepare the meals yourself. The only restaurants worth your money are fast-food stands attached to car washes. One knows that going to dinner with CJ and Johnny means hitting one of those car washes. They are especially fond of the Mexican food stand connected to the car wash on Vermont and Prospect, which—even I grudgingly admit—is pretty good. The four of us are so hungry we decide to eat on the plastic picnic tables next to the stand.

I get my food from the window first, and it is almost painful having to wait for everybody else to begin eating. To distract myself I look at an old car with a rusted-out hood parked nearby. The car was just shut off; the engine was overheating. Fluorescent green coolant bubbles up from corroded fissures in the hood and pools on the asphalt below like primordial goo brewing the first molecules of life.

We eat quickly when everyone gets their food and then head back to the house to get ready. CJ makes the three of us cocktails; he barely drinks himself.

CJ's outfit is cavewoman chic: a big red beehive with a bone stuck through it and a cocktail dress made of faux fur. She is a glamorous Flintstone wife in high-heeled boots. CJ mixes Johnny's drink extra strong, since Johnny quickly loses his inhibitions when drunk; by the time Johnny has drunk a quarter of the cocktail, CJ can dress him up as she pleases, fashioning him into her best Paleolithic girlfriend. She has a little trouble accessorizing Johnny to the requisite level of fabulousness, since clumsy Johnny needs to be kept in prosaic flats rather than fierce heels. In desperation, she finally gives Johnny the jewelry she was planning to wear herself, the ultimate Neanderthal bling: a choker and dangly earrings fashioned from hewn chunks of granite. CJ keeps the matching tennis bracelet for herself.

CJ winds Nathan in a fur toga and gives him a necklace with some sort of fang stung on it. I don't want to wear a costume.

"At least take your shirt off and let me put some body paint on you," says CJ.

"I'm not sure."

"You are going to take your shirt off anyway. Are you all waxed?"

"Yes."

"Good, then let me see some skin."

On my bicep and shoulder blade CJ reproduces a few cave paintings, bison and horse from Lascaux. Even I have to admit it looks pretty hot.

Most of the drag queens at the club are dressed like CJ and Johnny, but a few have stylized outfits inspired by prehistoric reptiles or saber-toothed cats. I usually don't drink much when I go out, but because CJ drove and I am having a good time with Nathan, I have a few gin and tonics. I dance a lot. Everything anyone says is either a hilarious joke or a sexy flirtation. The stage is decorated with giant tree ferns and a volcano with spewing lava that glows under the club's black lights. It is an enchanted world to me.

My phone rings—Travis. I can barely hear him over the music. He says something about trouble with Denise's costume.

"Are you on your way?" I shout.

He says yes but keeps going on about something she is wearing. I can't make out what he is saying.

"But you'll be here soon."

He says yes.

"We'll take care of it then."

He starts talking fast again, and I miss everything.

"We'll just take care of it when you get here," I shout a second time. "Hurry or you will miss CJ's performance."

He hangs up.

CJ is backstage. Nathan, Johnny and I are having so much fun on the dance floor that it isn't even awkward when Ron and Allan show up. I just hug them both and offer to get them a drink. I was just about to go to the bar anyway.

When I get back I compliment them on their costumes: Ron is in cavewoman drag and carries a big club to keep caveman Allan in line. Allan just wears a hide loincloth. They are planning to take part in the drag-queen parade and have been practicing a little routine: Ron will pretend to club Allan, throw him over his shoulder, and carry him across the stage—an inversion of that outdated, misogynistic cartoon cliché where the caveman captures a wife and drags her home by her hair.

After a few more songs the DJ announces that all the participants in the drag queen parade need to start assembling backstage. Johnny, Ron, and Allan leave to secure their places in the parade. Left alone, Nathan and I are making out as much as dancing. Nathan runs his fingertips over my skin.

"Don't smudge my bison," I say in a low voice. He keeps touching me, and I try not to get a hard-on.

Travis finally finds us in the crowd and breaks Nathan and me up. He looks frazzled. He put his costume together himself: a leopard-print bathrobe he bought at Goodwill—which he assumed would make him look like a caveman—worn over a white wife-beater and a pair of corduroys. Inexplicably, he chose to wear his horn-rimmed glasses rather than his contacts. More than a caveman, he looks like James Dean, had he lived long enough to hang out at the Playboy Mansion.

"Denise is taking part in the drag-queen parade," he says.

"She is dressed like a man dressed like I woman?" I say, trying to understand Travis's panic.

"CJ is going to be pissed."

I tell him to relax. What, after all, could really offend a room full of drunken drag queens?

"OK, you'll just have to see it to appreciate the situation."

The show starts.

The emcee drag queen emerges from behind the volcano and greets the crowd. She wears a sequined jumpsuit and cape, colored magenta with chartreuse spots like a cartoon dinosaur. The high ruffled collar of the cape and the three horns rising out of her wig are fashioned to look like a triceratops head.

Through a campy, circuitous monologue she breaks the news that one of the drag queens who was supposed to perform tonight was injured and is convalescing at home. While practicing her routine, "Cavebootylicious," on her lanai, she slipped on an ice cube thrown at her by an angry neighbor. Clearly this neighbor was a "philistine, a man with no appreciation for an artiste at work."

Everyone moans with overdramatic despair at the news, but Lady Triceratops tells them to perk up because a new drag queen, the fabulous CJ has stepped up and adopted one of her routines for tonight's show.

The music starts, and CJ comes out singing his own version of Nina Simone's "Feeling Good." She tweaked some of the words to make them fit the evening:

> *Brontosaurus in the swamp, you know how I feel*
> *Pterodactyl in the sky, you know how I feel*
> *Magma spewing from the earth, you know how I feel*
>
> *It's a new world*
> *It's a new age*
> *It's the Stone Age*
> *For me*
> *And I'm feeling good*

The thing is, her voice is so huge and her delivery is so confident that nobody is paying attention to the strangeness of her lyrics. The crowd goes crazy when she finishes.

"How does that huge voice come out of that guy?" asks Nathan when the applause dies down.

Travis and I agree that we've never heard her sing like that before.

Lady Triceratops comes out to introduce the next performer and falls into another lengthy monologue. "Birds sing to attract mates; moose bellow for love. I saw a nature documentary about tigers—they have real problems because they are so solitary—cats

175

wander the jungle for days making this plaintive cry, looking for a lady tiger. You can bet primitive man was no different. When the cave people convened to think up the first words, they weren't brainstorming to come up with 'fire,' 'boulder,' and 'hit mastodon with club.' You know they were figuring out how to say, 'Hey baby, you look hot! Want to get it on?' The first words were 'tits' and 'cock' and 'ass.' If our language preserves its past in buried layers, there is an eroticism at its core that we must key into at some level."

Lady Triceratops becomes annoyed at the giggling coming from some of the crowd: "You may laugh at me and see me as a chunky middle-aged man in a wig and a sequined bodysuit who knows nothing of such things, but I tell you that modern media has you tricked. Sex is not only for the young or beautiful. It is a part of each of us, as we are part of the unbroken chain leading back to the first cell in the primeval seas. If you split open my head, you will find a kama sutra endlessly propagating itself, an endless loop, the infinite variety."

With that, Lady Triceratops introduces Triassica Lee performing a disco routine about walking over the land bridge during the last ice age. Triassica Lee does not have CJ's voice, but her dance moves are innovative, especially one that combines the Shuffle with a pantomime of chipping a Clovis point from flint.

The drag-queen parade follows Triassica Lee's performance. It is an opportunity for all the costumed attendees to take part in a procession across the stage: each taking her turn to strut out from behind the volcano, do a few dance moves among the tree ferns, and blow kisses at the cheering crowd. While the drag queen has her moment on stage, Lady Triceratops, Triassica Lee, and CJ make witty—but never mean—comments about her outfit. A leggy drag queen, obviously a dancer, does a few twirls and then falls to the floor in full splits; the commentators agree that after a display of such limberness she will certainly get lucky by the end of the night. Johnny stumbles out, looks a little dazed in the spotlights, kisses CJ's hand, and sheepishly hurries off the stage—obviously not one for an over-the-top display of show-woman ship.

Then Denise comes out. Choosing between a cavewoman or an ancient beast to inspire her costume, she opted for the latter. With an audacious, ostrich-feather-topped hat, long folds of cloth hanging below her arms like wings, and more plumes hanging behind her as a tail, it was not obvious exactly what ancient beast she might be. At minimum, she is an extravagant, extinct creature in variegated taffeta. They announce her as Mistress Archaeopteryx. Past that, the commentators are speechless. When I suggested to Denise that she test-drive bigger breasts, this club was not the arena I had in mind. But Mistress Archaeopteryx's bust is so obviously padded into exaggerated boobs that she easily passes for a drag queen. The liberal application of makeup helps too. Half a dozen different colors of eye shadow on each eyelid create a pattern with the complexity of a butterfly wing.

The brim of her hat and the hem of her wings catch the spotlights and shine like jewels. To add this extra sparkle to her costume, I think she may have sewn on giant rhinestones or drop-shaped prisms or some other shinny baubles. Then I realize what they are. Denise has attached dozens of the tiny crystal dinosaurs from Pick-N-Save to her dress.

I look at Travis. He nods his head. Yes, this is what he had been trying to tell me on the phone. I look back at the stage. CJ is taciturn. The other two commentators recover from their initial confusion about Denise's costume and make jokes about the shimmying bird before them.

Ron and Allan are next in the parade, so they have certainly seen the dinosaurs as well. Although their dominant cavewoman shtick gets some chuckles, it lacks the theatricality of which they are capable. They are obviously vexed by seeing scores of the dinosaurs they had been told were expensive and greatly coveted in Japan stitched in so profligate a manner into Denise's dress. Could they believe this was a coincidence, or had Denise told them about hearing the story of the thrift-store dinos from me? Obviously, she was not a woman to hold her tongue.

"I'm so dead," I say to Travis.

Indeed, Johnny, CJ, Ron, and Allan piece together the whole plot backstage. Johnny is upset about looking cheap and getting caught in a petty deception. Ron and Allan are looking for any excuse to get mad at me again. CJ just feels betrayed. He feels betrayed that I would make him and his partner look so bad to someone outside our group and break our circle of confidences. I don't think he would have been the least bothered had I shown up decked in dinosaurs to expose the charade. He would be the first to laugh at his boyfriend's frugality. He feels hurt I shared the information with someone who is barely an acquaintance while withholding it from him. I had gone outside the tribe.

This all blows up after the drag show, on the club's patio. Enough alcohol has absorbed into my blood for events to register as discrete images rather than a coherent narrative: Johnny breaking away from the general argument to dance alone atop a chair, only to fall off the chair and into some bushes; CJ bitching me out as only a drag queen can bitch someone out; Johnny's wig askew as he rises from the bushes and bums a cigarette from a man who refers to himself in the third person as the "Penis-Saurus Rex"; a few guys stopping to compliment my torso adorned like a cave wall; Travis in his second-hand bathrobe, trying to mollify CJ and Allan and be the peacemaker; Nathan moving his hands down my abdomen and just below the waistband of my jeans.

"I think the three of us should probably leave," says Travis. Nathan stops kissing my neck. Drunk as I am, I know Travis is right.

"I was going to say good-bye to Denise, but she is drunk herself and dancing in the middle of a ring of gay guys. I think I'm done with her. We better call a cab," he says.

As we are walking out, Travis stops to get the number of a cab company from the coat-check guy. The short man with the Mohawk, who is always at these things taking pictures, snaps of photo of the three of us while we stand outside by the valet, waiting for the cab to arrive.

12

ALLAN AND RON ARE MAD AT ME for writing the defamatory
email, Johnny and CJ are mad at me for gossiping to Denise
about the dubious origins of the glass dinosaur, Lucinda is so
irate about my involvement with Nathan and Travis that she will
not return my calls—so all my time away from work is spent with
Nathan and Travis.

Nathan comes by my apartment after his rehearsal finishes
on Friday, and we drive to Travis's loft to pick him up for dinner.
Like me, Travis has withdrawn from all company besides Nathan
and me. Unlike me, his seclusion is voluntary rather than the result of
being shunned. When not with Nathan or me, he works on his new
sculptures. Gone are his urban peregrinations, gone are meditation
and sleep. He works on a diet of herbal tea, dehydrated fruit, and rice
cakes, leaving the loft only to purchase supplies.

I got some idea of the long hours Travis was working when,

last weekend, he fell asleep on my couch while the three of us were watching a movie. He snored and drool trickled from his open mouth. I had never seen Travis so unguarded. Only now, when I see his loft filled with new sculptures, do I realize the full extent of his recent labors. Free standing pieces dominate the room, but a couple mobiles also hang from the ceiling. Other works are mounted to the walls. Just months ago this space was empty.

I call the restaurant to cancel our reservations and have food delivered instead. Despite the drop cloths and nails that liter the floor, the band saw standing off to the side, the turpentine fumes, the sanders and drills plugged into every electrical outlet, the loft is a gallery for us tonight. Travis walks Nathan and me around the sculptures, giving us a private tour. Many pieces are only partially completed, so Travis explains how he intends to finish these works. Travis's sculptures explore the concept and meaning of home. Many sculptures assemble construction materials—cabinetry, double-paned windows, tile, and latex-covered drywall—into abstract shapes with no utility, keeping only the rectilinear design typical of our dwellings and cities. Other pieces invite you to walk either inside or under them, only to force you to question whether they are sheltering you or entrapping you. A bower, for example, has PVC piping and electrical wire on the outside and stucco and shingles on the inside. Another work has a conventional interior: paint on the walls, parquet floors, and lights hanging from the ceiling—that slowly constricts the further you walk into it, until you are crawling in what still appears to be a hallway built to proper scale. Travis encourages us to sit inside the cardboard shipping box from a Subzero refrigerator, which he has lined with marble. A second box from another large appliance sits next to it, outfitted with a Spanish-style tile roof. It is the beginning of a piece he calls "McMansion Subdivision." He is looking for more boxes to complete the piece; one he will equip, perhaps, with a flat-screen TV.

Travis chooses to go back to my apartment with Nathan and me. He says he needs to get away from the loft lest he keep working and not get the sleep he obviously needs. Travis quickly retires to the spare bedroom and encourages Nathan and me to have our fun without him. I do not think Travis can hear Nathan and me having sex—or even wants to—but I suspect part of him needs Nathan and me to be fucking, needs to be in the apartment for this ritual of the two of us retreating behind my bedroom door, emerging the next morning to have breakfast with him. Travis smiles when I kiss him on the top of the head as I walk by, joining him for breakfast at the kitchen table where he is already seated, sketching out some ideas for new sculptures.

It isn't me but Travis who brings up the beach over breakfast. He reminds us how on our first meeting last winter he had sheepishly told Nathan we would take him to the nude beach in Santa Barbara if there was warm weather in spring.

"Before you got up," says Travis, "I checked the weather forecast on the computer. This heat wave is supposed to last through Thursday."

"I can't go this weekend," says Nathan. The quartet is driving to La Jolla this afternoon for a recital tonight and another recital tomorrow afternoon. These concerts are the end of the group's SoCal performances; they are leaving early Wednesday morning.

Travis says he remembered the recitals but thought there might be a way to go Monday or Tuesday. It all depends on me.

"There is no way I can go on Monday." I say, "I've got my group meeting Monday morning, plus I am teaching Monday and Wednesday afternoons this semester." I check my schedule for Tuesday. I have a couple of meetings with students Tuesday morning, but they are nothing urgent and can be rescheduled for later in the week. I had Tuesday afternoon blocked off for working on a grant, but I can just work in the evenings after Nathan leaves. I say that I don't like to make a habit of canceling on students, but I can reschedule my meetings and go to the beach on Tuesday. It is a special occasion. I ask Travis if he is sure the weather will be good, and he assures me it will be in the nineties and sunny.

Nathan is excited. "This is so awesome. This is the perfect going-away present. I'll just do my packing on Monday. If we get back late on Tuesday, who cares? I'll just stay up all night and sleep on the plane."

I am a little concerned. "You remember, Travis, this is a nude beach. Are you sure you are OK with that?"

"I'm not promising to take off my clothes, but I promise I'll be fine when you two do."

"It will probably be deserted, anyway, midweek in spring," I say, "and there are usually some people who are in swimsuits rather than being totally nude."

I tell them about the first time I went to a nude beach. It was in Santa Barbara. Not the Meditation Beach (properly, More Mesa) where we are going on Tuesday, but down in Summerland. I was nervous, naturally, and it was the summer before my ex-boyfriend moved to Santa Barbara to be with me, so I was going to the beach alone. I found it easily enough; dozens of naked people on a beach are difficult to miss. I spread out my towel on the edge of the crowd, quickly pulled off my bathing suit, and lay down without looking around. I felt the sun warming my whole body. I stuck my head up and watched the waves. It was just a short time until I chilled out, realized the beauty of all this, and decided it would be judicious to rub on some sunscreen.

A naked guy in his mid-fifties with a CB radio walked up to me, introduced himself, and explained that he was one of the unofficial chiefs of the beach's naked people. He explained that the truce between the naked people and the Santa Barbara sheriffs was predicated on no nude people being visible to motorists on Interstate 101. I had positioned myself slightly too far north and needed to move a few yards down the beach, into the mass of nakedness.

I talked to him a little while and learned that he had lived here for decades, in a house at the top of the cliffs. He and his friends were trying to keep the beach free for nudity. He told me about sheriff raids in the past, in which officers risked breaking their own necks by rushing down the near vertical cliffs to catch nude sunbathers by surprise. Meanwhile, other officers on jet skis would ride in from the ocean and help surround the beachgoers in a coordinated strike. For the moment the authorities were practicing confinement, but there was nothing stopping them from deciding to raid the beach again. The naked elders used radios to try to warn each other if there was any sign of an attack descending on the nudists. Hopefully, with some warning, people could get their clothes on in time to avoid being fined.

Only when I moved into the crowd did I appreciate the nude beach's spirit: naked people of all ages, naked elderly reading Sunday papers and naked toddlers digging in the sand, the sleek and toned, the overweight and sagging, men and women playing volleyball nude, tossing Frisbees nude, groups of gay guys hanging out and chatting nude. There was nothing sexual about the beach; it was more like a gleeful pagan version of paradise.

The sheriff closed down the nude beach at Summerland two summers after my first visit there. The rumor was that pressure from upscale tourists doomed the nude beach—probably the aged baby boomers covering self-hatred with outrage when confronted with a living symbol of their old ideals and the impossibility of reconciling those ideals with their six-hundred-dollar hotel rooms and Lexus SUVs. The Meditation Beach was thankfully left alone.

Nathan looks at me incredulously. "Seriously, are you telling me a bunch of gay dudes are getting together naked and there are no tawdry liaisons going on?"

"Like everything," I reply, "it's what you make of it. For me, the beach was all about the vibe, but if you are looking for it, the hookups are there. The Meditation Beach has more of a sleazy side than Summerland, because it is more secluded. You park in this suburban area, then walk quite a ways across a plateau of coastal chaparral, until you come to the top of the cliffs where you first see the ocean through the eucalyptus trees. After going down a long series of steps to the beach, it is clothed people to the left of the steps and nude people to the right. Turning right, it is mainly hetero nudes at first. The further you go, the gayer it gets. After about a mile the beach turns to rocks, and if you keep going into the rocks it definitely becomes a gay cruising zone. I never did anything there. For me the beach is about being intimate with nature, with nothing separating you from the water, sun, and earth. I guess it is as close to spiritual as I get."

Even after hearing that, when Nathan and I are alone in my bedroom, he whispers to me that he wants us to sneak away from Travis at the beach so I can fuck him. "My first boyfriend in Oregon and I would drive to the beach at night and mess around in the sand. It has been forever since I've gotten to do that."

"I thought your first boyfriend was in London."

"That was my first love, not my first boyfriend. I was an insatiable, randy bottom in high school."

This is all overdetermined: Nathan's plea for a fuck on the beach is probably a genuine attempt to recapture a memory of his high school days in America, but it is also part of a game, a dare to see if he can coax me into having sex somewhere he knows I would prefer not to. I have realized by this point in the affair that sex for

Nathan is largely a game, trading moves and positions that we've picked up over the years, trying to deplete each other's repertoire, and also seeing how far outside my comfort zone he can push me. My motives are as mixed as his. My pride is partially responsible for keeping me from opting out of this particular game, but (admittedly) any game that involves having this kind of sex with someone this beautiful is not a game from which I will quickly walk away.

And if familiarity created by the weeks of seeing Nathan naked has blunted my appreciation of his beauty, Nathan walking out of the Pacific at the Meditation Beach (the water so cold this time of year that I wouldn't join him swimming) reminds me again how his body recalls that small Greek statue's idealization of the athletic male form. I become hard instantly. After emerging from the surf, Nathan walks directly up to me and extends his hand as a signal for me to rise up from my towel, and I do. I say nothing, but Nathan looks over his shoulder as we walk away and tells Travis that we will be right back. I should feel awkward about the hard-on in front of Travis, but I let Nathan lead me over the rocks to the adjoining secluded cove without embarrassment.

Nathan lies in the sand and pulls me atop him. Not one to be beat without a good fight, I do not rush to give Nathan what he wants. Rather than hasten the end of something with which I am uncomfortable, I prolong everything. I spare no time kissing Nathan, licking his nipples, spare no time caressing his chest and thighs.

He pulls his legs apart and arches his butt up, but I ignore his genitals and his ass. I spend an eternity sucking the sensitive skin between his testicles and his ass and a second eternity on the tender crease where his testicles meet his leg. And then I move slowly outward, nibbling the inside of his thigh. And then I do the same to the other leg. And then I start again with the first. It is something that drove me insane when my ex-boyfriend would do it to me, something I have saved up to use on Nathan. Eventually, he is so crazed he throws me down, sits on my hard-on, and fucks himself.

When we make our way around the rocks to return to the towels, I see Travis standing down the beach, without a shirt, letting the white water lap at his feet. I put my hand on Nathan's chest to stop him from walking further, and I watch Travis. He runs away from a particularly large wave and then runs back into the water when the wave recedes. He bends down and splashes the water with his hands, and the sun glitters against the thousands of drops he creates in that single motion. Even from this far away I can see him smiling. At this moment, more than anything, I want to walk over and hug him.

Travis eventually sees Nathan and me and motions us back. Since the beach outing was Travis's idea, he insisted that he pack our lunch. He bought fresh strawberries, the fat ones you can only get at farmer's markets in spring, and wrapped them in paper towels to keep them from being bruised. We drink blood-orange juice he squeezed this morning, and we eat baguettes he loaded with artichoke hearts, roasted red peppers, and smoked mozzarella cheese. We snack on pita chips dipped in humus and eat more strawberries for dessert. After finishing Nathan's going-away feast, we recline together on the beach towels, napping and talking, for the rest of the afternoon, watching the sun go down on the otherwise deserted beach.

NATHAN LEAVES UNCEREMONIOUSLY the next morning. In my now-quiet condo I think longingly of Travis during the subsequent days, but not until Saturday do I call him and go over to his loft where he is staining wood for one of his sculptures. I make myself tea, waiting for him to finish; we make small talk about the progress of "McMansion Subdivision."

When he can take a break, we sit outside and drink our tea. Not being particularly good at subtlety, I blurt out, "Travis, do you think you could ever be happy with me, romantically, in a relationship? This time with you and Nathan has been the happiest for me in forever. You know, if you just give me the word, I'll drop everything for you. You and I could just get away from here. You could do your art, and I could teach at a community college somewhere."

Travis puts his fingers to my lips to stop me from talking. He tells me he will never, ever, have sex with me. "Did you think our three-way fling would continue? Or turn into a relationship between you and me?"

He stares at me, waiting for an answer to his question. I feel cold all over.

"Why are you trying to make me feel bad? You are the one who suggested all this," I say.

"All I suggested is that you and Nathan have sex," he replies.

I am very upset. Travis sees that and says, "Don't get like that,

Damon. I'm in a much worse position than you. I cannot lose your friendship. Can't you see it? I need you so much more than you need me."

"What do you mean by that?"

"You like food. You like music, science, art, and the pleasures of the flesh. Whatever happens, you will be fine in the end. Unlike you, however, my place in this world is so fragile."

Unearthing his feelings to me seems to cause Travis physical pain; he shakes like an exhausted runner trying to finish a marathon. Despite this, he continues, "Most of the people you are around are just like you—you've said it yourself—they have parents who are scientists, engineers, or doctors, and they went to good high schools and universities and probably played on youth soccer teams on the weekend and joined junior lifeguards in the summer. That is not where I'm from, Damon. You cannot understand how jarring it is to look around and see where I am now. I don't even know if the emotion has a name. What do you call a combination of terror and gratitude? The kids around me when I was young, at best they went to junior college, got some girl pregnant, and are working at a tire store to pay child support. The chasm I feel is getting wider and wider since I've been on TV. On one hand, I get stopped on the street for autographs and get calls about writing my own book about do-it-yourself home projects. On the other hand, every time I hear about a childhood acquaintance, they are either dead or destitute. I need you, Damon. I need your friendship to live. You are an anchor to me, a bridge. I can't risk losing that."

"You already put everything on the line. You risked everything for this crazy relationship," I say.

"What is different between you and me? What is different between now and before we met Nathan? Nothing is different, absolutely nothing."

"How can you say that?"

"Damon, you got to have sex with a guy you were salivating over since the first moment you saw him, and I got to pretend for a short time that I am more normal than I really am."

"So you think that is all this was? Me having sex and you role-playing at a real relationship?"

"Yes," he says.

"I love you. How can you say all this when I love you?"

"You probably do, Damon, but that is not the issue. It is not that I don't love you, it is that I can't. Not you or anyone. Not in the way you are talking about; it just isn't in my programming. I'm not going to join an order of monks and take a vow of celibacy just to give it a name and make it more palatable. I'm alone and can't be with anybody else."

"What is wrong with you?" I nearly shout this, and immediately feel guilty.

"This isn't easy for me," says Travis, barely in a whisper.

Travis takes my hand. "I'm leaving to start filming the new season of the show soon, and you are going to Europe. You will just be angry and confused for a time. It will pass. I'll come back after filming in the autumn, and it will again be just as it always has between us. And face it, Damon, how much of this stuff is even about me or Nathan, and how much of it is about Felix anyway?"

After that, there doesn't seem like anything more needs to be said. So I leave.

13

WIRE FENCES AND POWER LINES mark the border between Austria and Hungary. In America we might see the fall of the Berlin Wall as emblematic of Central Europe's liberation from communism, but it began properly here, two months before the events in Berlin, when the Hungarian government authorized East German tourists vacationing in Hungary to leave for the West, where asylum in West Germany awaited them. The first break in the Iron Curtain was somewhere in this chain-link fence. Even though it is summer, the midweek train between Vienna and Budapest is relatively empty. Austrian soldiers depart at the border, and the other passengers are British tourists, judging from their accents. A Hungarian official steps into the car to stamp passports, and I mistakenly give him my train ticket rather than my passport. I don't speak German, but it was easy enough to pick up a dozen phrases during my week in Austria. Even at the conference, where

English was the common language among international scientists, the preponderance of German-speaking researchers allowed me to increase my small vocabulary during casual chats. German has a perceptible form, even when the content is incomprehensible. The Hungarian spoken by the border guard, in contrast, lacks any pattern to my ears, slipping away like a fluid through parted fingers. I give him my passport after my initial confusion and then sit back in my seat. Deeper into the Little Hungarian Plain, poppies stretch away from the tracks. As a Californian, I presuppose wild poppies should be orange, so the accompaniment of these crimson flowers makes the passage east feel slightly uncanny.

I am staying at Nathan's apartment near Kálvin Square during my week vacation in Budapest. He is with the quartet in Tokyo. I hesitated at first to accept his offer to use the apartment, wanting to put all the events between him, Travis, and me behind me. Frugality, however, won out in the end. And also a realization that there is no reason for Nathan and me not to remain friends, other than my own residual discomfort with my actions in the last several months, actions which are, in the end, certainly no fault of Nathan's.

Arriving at Keleti Station, I take the subway to Kálvin Square rather than a taxi, to better acquaint myself with moving around the city. The jolly neighbor with whom Nathan leaves his keys shows me into the apartment. He gives me a quick introduction both to the gay scene in Budapest, marking his favorite clubs on my city map with stars, and to the city's history, encouraging me to lean awkwardly out a small window to see how the apartment is built right into the old city wall of one of Pest's medieval incarnations. He leaves after fifteen minutes to get back to his midday beer and laundry.

Walking to the river after settling myself in the apartment, the eagle-capped spires of the Szabadság Bridge, an ornate cast-iron bridge painted copper-oxide-green, are the first signs of the city's elegance. During my week in Budapest it is this bridge, rather than the iconic, lion-guarded Chain Bridge, that I adopt as my favorite piece of Magyar architecture. I eventually learn that it is not an eagle at each apex of the bridge, but a turul, a great bird that engendered the Magyar in the mythic past.

The banks of the Danube in central Budapest seem more like an idealization of what a Central European capital should look like than a real city: Mátyás Church and Buda Palace echo Vienna's Stephansdom and Schönbrunn, but here they are placed more audaciously atop a hill overlooking the river. The temporary escape afforded by a flower-planted urban park is accentuated here by placing that park on an island unto itself in the middle of the Danube. The parliament building, placed photogenically on the river bank, is larger than even Westminster Palace in London. In this perpetually bombed and besieged city, most of these landmarks have been repeatedly rebuilt. The present Mátyás Church, for example, contains only a small portion of the original thirteenth-century structure. The church was rebuilt following the siege that banished the Ottomans in the seventeenth century and again following fighting between the Germans and the Russians that ruined Castle Hill in the twentieth century.

The Budapest underground, which is the oldest subway system on the continent, has a ticketing system with a labyrinthine logic incomprehensible to the non-Magyar: day passes, three-day passes, week passes, passes that allow you to ride for three stops, passes that allow you to ride for five stops and may include one transfer, passes that allow you to make as many transfers as you want as long as you continue traveling in the same direction, passes that allow you to ride for as long as you want on a single line as long as you make no transfers. Transit security squads roam the underground, check passes, and fine violators on the spot. I thought my week pass was fail-safe, until one ticket checker pointed out that I never signed the back of the pass. I had never even turned it over to notice it needed signing. I also soon realized that the security squads always check tourists, assuming they are the most likely ones to mess up the pass system. Not even being white, it is useless for me to attempt to pass as a Hungarian, no matter how I dress or carry myself. I've accepted the fact that my pass will be checked every time I ride the subway.

My mornings in Budapest begin with coffee and toast in the apartment. The Central Market is steps away, so I stock the refrigerator with produce, mild cheese, and paprika salami. I pack a picnic into my messenger bag most days and set out to walk the city, putting the mess I left in LA behind me for a time, stopping to eat in a park when I feel hungry, grabbing a cappuccino at a café mid-afternoon, swimming late in the afternoon at one of the city's many baths. I stop by Chaos most evenings, not for the stylish basement bar but for the street-level Internet café where I can check email.

Most are for work, of course, but I am messaging back and forth with Lucinda, both of us apologizing for our blowup. It is an email from Russ on my next-to-last day in Budapest, however, that leaves me confused:

Damon,

The attached file is a letter I handwrote months ago and just scanned to a PDF. I know I am a coward for sending it to you electronically while you are on another continent rather than delivering it to you by hand. As I explain inside, I've been restraining my feelings for some time because I knew the depth of your heartbreak in the wake of the split with your ex-boyfriend. None of my feelings have changed since I wrote this letter, only now my longing for you has become more acute in light of your three-way relationship thing. I never felt threatened by your frisky carousing since I knew it amounted to nothing. This three-way thing was something different, something your heart was somehow attached to. If nothing has happened since our one drunken night, I suspect nothing ever will. But faced with the option of regret over never communicating my love or the option of pain after your probable rejection, I choose the latter. I spoke to Lucinda about this, finally. She urged me to remove this weight from my chest.

Sincerely,

Russell

The PDF letter is long, so I ask the staff for help printing it out, and go to a nearby café where I read it over a pizza (oddly, with corn kernels atop it) and a glass of Magyar red wine.

Dear Damon,

I'm writing you this letter on the flight from Sydney to Los Angeles after two weeks in Australia for my older sister's wedding. I'm not certain you will ever see these words; I suspect this is one of those letters you write in order to clarify your thoughts, with no intention of mailing it to the addressee.

My parents, younger sister, and I spent most of these two weeks at a beach house in Avoca Beach, a couple hours north of Sydney by train, where my older sister's fiancé's—now, husband's—family lives. The ceremony was on a sand dune in front of the beach house, and the reception was at the fiancé's family's house in Gosford. Maybe I can blame my emotions on being surrounded by talk of family and of weddings for a fortnight. Certainly the awkwardness of being one of the only single people at a reception full of couples also contributed to this rush of feelings. Admittedly, however, there is also a dash of sexual frustration fueling this, after being surrounded for two weeks by shirtless Aussie guys in this very hetero beach town.

The beach house sits on a small lake separated from the ocean by maybe

50 yards of sand, and the beach itself is maybe a mile long. One day I walked north across the hills to the next town, Terrigal. Halfway, there was a headland overlooking the Tasman Sea from which you could see the coastline in both directions—rocky, eucalyptus-capped points alternating with sandy beaches stretching to either horizon. What it must have been like to live here as one of the first people.

One day midweek my younger sister and I took the train to Sydney to see the Royal Botanic Gardens and Bondi Beach. During the train ride the ocean seemed to be on either side of the car at various times due to all the bays, lagoons, and inlets—and Sydney was just as confusing with the same filigreed coastline, the Botanic Gardens occupying one of the many peninsulas. Things sublime and sinister filled the garden: flying foxes hang from the taller trees, languidly beating their wings in the heat; there was this one pine found by a bushwhacker in 1994 that was previously known only from the fossil record and a palm from Hawaii, only twelve of which are known to exist; colonies of three-inch long spiders building reticulated supra-webs formed from the intersecting planes of their individual webs; black-and-white birds with long beaks and legs (ibis? storks?) common as seagulls; and everywhere couples knotted together on the endless lawns.

I could have just stayed in the gardens, but my sister wanted to see the Opera House (the roof of which seems to be covered with interlocking bathroom tile, on close inspection), and she wanted to see the Rocks (hot and tourist congested, crowds gathered to watch an Aborigine man in dreads and body paint play the theme from "The Godfather" on tin drums), and she wanted to marvel at the luxury homes lining the bay and decide which belonged to Nicole Kidman and which belonged to Russell Crowe. But there are young Aussie men everywhere—muscular, shorts nearly falling off their waists—so I consent to go with my sister and keep myself occupied watching the guys.

And Bondi is just ridiculous—an arc of the tan, fit youth of the world. English, Scandinavian and Asian tongues float about us, and there are more topless women than I've seen in a long time. I was too enamored with it all to be self-conscious about my slight frame; I lay back and buried my hands in the warm sand at my sides. Unfortunately, Aussie men do not age well—a diet of beer and sun means at too early an age they simultaneously swell and wrinkle.

One night in the beach house when everybody but me was asleep, I sat on the back patio and watched the night sky. To see more stars I needed to get away from the lights of the town so I jumped the back fence and walked to the beach; I went far down the empty sand to find the darkness I wanted. I only remember seeing the Milky Way once before in my life, during a family vacation to Hawaii when I was eleven. I don't know the constellations, but I could find Orion (the only one visible in LA, right?), although down there he was standing on his head. He was far in the northern sky, and I realized this was the first time I could have seen most of the stars in the half of the sky below him. I tried to find the Southern Cross, but there were innumerable sets of four stars that formed crosses. I remembered the Australian flag and the extra star on the left crossbar, but

I couldn't find that pattern anywhere above me. Seated out there alone, I started thinking about how I didn't want to be alone. Damon, it was you I wanted by my side, you with whom I wanted to be searching the stars, you with whom I wanted to be exploring this coastline.

One afternoon on the beach I saw what appeared to be small balloons—kidney shaped and maybe five or six centimeters long. They collapsed when I handled them, or flew out of my fingers in the wind. I thought they were seaweed floats, but the next day the tide brought schools of them ashore, with the tentacles still attached, the lifeguards driving up and down the beach ordering on their loudspeakers for all swimmers to leave the water. Only then did I realize that yesterday's balloons were jellyfish dried in the sun, the fragile tentacles dehydrated and destroyed before I had gotten to the beach. "Blue Bottles," the lifeguards called them. I stayed out of the water for the rest of the day. They also found a dying sea snake on the edge of the lake one day—one of those black-and-white-banded snakes whose venom is the most lethal on the planet. Some of the wildlife was less fearsome—I finally saw a kookaburra after hearing the calls for days, and one night, going out to investigate a rattling by the trash cans, I glimpsed a plump possum escaping to the roof.

I liked the beach best at the end of the day—joggers, dog walkers, and surfers became more prevalent as the falling sun created mottled patterns of shadows in the footprint-pocked sand. Weekday afternoons were good, too, when the whaleboat (dragon boat? lifeguard boat?) practiced on the lake. The coach manning the rudder wore a T-shirt and board shorts, but the four paddlers wore the smallest of matching Speedos. From the neck down all four men were identical—same tanned skin, same long frame, same hairless chest, twinning each other on opposite sides of the boat.

I spent two days back in Sydney at the end of the trip and felt like I was already back in Southern California—the vibe felt like LA or San Diego, and the city looked like San Francisco. I missed Mardi Gras by one week, but I did get tickets for the Harbor Party, a circuit party back in the Botanic Gardens with views of the Opera House and the Harbor Bridge. My older sister introduced me to some of her gay friends, and I spent the evening with them. We danced in the middle of the crowd, all the Aussie men with their shirts off now. I couldn't take my eyes off this tall, fit guy, a little older, his hair just graying (it would have been dyed in LA) who had half a tattoo (maybe a sea turtle?) peeking over the bright waistband of his briefs, which, of course, rode up above his jeans. As the sun set a procession of dancers entered, two by two. Some were dressed like pixies, with antenna and wings, some dressed like satyrs, with their heads and arms wrapped with vines. The pixies tossed glitter as they promenaded through the crowd.

For three hours it drizzled, warm drops dangling frozen in the pulsing lasers, the skin of the jostling guys around me slick with water. After a diva sang a generic dance anthem, the rain started in for real. I was so soaked, I could feel water pouring down my legs beneath my jeans. Finally, it became too cold, and the group I was with decided to leave. They were going to party all night, but I went back to my hotel. There were no cabs so I walked, drenched gay boys fanning out from the gardens into the city.

I filled the bath with warm water to heat myself up. My journey to Australia fell short of anything serious and engravable, but it did help me clarify my feelings towards you. I've been trying to respect the fact that you are going through a lot of anguish after your breakup and need to work through that anguish before anything can be possible between us. I am really expecting—as it seems so naïve when I put it into words— that I will receive a succinct voicemail from you one day soon, saying something like, "Russ, I'm over my shit. I can love you now. I'll pick you up for dinner."

We are still warriors battling dragons. The serpents have only now made themselves invisible by depositing random events, the everyday mundane, upon their scales. We can still slay them in deeds worthy of legend, but slowly, one choice at a time. With every choice to watch TV alone rather than leave the house, with every time we choose lust over love, with every moment of self-pity, with every slip into decadence, their claws reach around us. We live in our small triumphs: to create, to think, to love, to reason. There are no breakthroughs and no epiphanies, just a series of small choices summed over years. Nothing seems forced between you and me when we are together, it feels like we just fall into step with one another. Part of me is confused why nothing happens between us. Why isn't this becoming a great love? To me it feels slow, inevitable, enduring.

I didn't even bother to shut the blinds when I fell asleep that last night in Sydney. When I awoke the next morning, I could see the neighboring building out the balcony's sliding door. On that building's roof, I saw a white bird the size of a condor. I thought the perspective must be off. Can you really expect to see a bird that size in the middle of a city? The roof opposite must be nearer than it appeared. But when I walked to the balcony I saw everything clearly—the roof was far away, and the preening bird was huge. The bird was white with a yellow crest, a cockatoo. I've seen them in zoos, but never like this, never this size. As much as I can fool myself into believing that this city could just as easily be in California, looking at this gargantuan feathery beast I think: what fucking insane island have I found myself upon?

Russell

My last day in Budapest I was intending to take a bus out to this park with Soviet-era statues rounded up from all over the city. Quite an ingenious way to deal with the horrible past: put it on display and charge admission. Instead, I go back to Hősök Square. Seven bronze men on horseback, representing the seven original tribes that founded Hungary, stand on the central plinth. I stand before this one tribal chieftain, Huba, who is so tough that even his horse wears a fearsome headdress made of elk antlers.

"Huba," I say, "did you ever have trouble with relationships?"

"Honestly," he responds, "we marauding hordes were more into picking up concubines in the lands we conquered. I can't say we really dated."

"I'm more into the guys," I say, "but that does sound hot."

"I guess I was just more focused on my professional life," he says. "I wasn't much of a family man."

"But you helped found a nation, isn't that sort of being the ultimate family man?"

"Maybe, but we didn't realize we were founding a nation. At the time I was only worried about providing my tribe land for grazing the livestock and securing shelter without the threat of enemy attacks. Everything was so difficult and uncertain. Who could have known that this place would be any different than the other lands we had tried to settle and were forced to flee? Who knew our fate would be different than the other nomadic tribes who disappeared from this earth without their names being recorded? Only in retrospect does it seem like we had a plan, that the plot seemed inevitable. But enough about me, why are you so troubled?"

"Maybe I lack the full palette of human emotions," I say. "Or maybe the love presented in movies and TV is so inaccurate that it makes me feel like a deficient person."

Huba furrows his brow and says that he doesn't really follow what I'm saying.

"I certainly feel sexually attracted to people I know only casually," I continue, "but love for me is never a sudden and rapturous thing. Not that, in time, my feelings are any less intense than anybody else's—they just need time to grow. The most perfect relationship could be right before me, but I need an initial kick to provide the activation energy."

I suddenly feel foolish talking about my guy problems with a warrior. I try to make a polite excuse for leaving, mindful of appearing rude to a guy who has a sword the thickness of my leg hanging from his saddle.

"Where are you going?" demands Huba. I never imagined barbarians as being so inquisitive.

"I have a long journey tomorrow, longer than you can even imagine: early-morning train from here to Vienna, then a flight from Vienna to Zurich, then a long flight from Zurich to Los Angeles."

"We've had successful raids against some of those places," he brags.

"Not the last one, I don't think. But anyway, I am on my way to the Széchenyi Baths. I am going to sit in the warm water and decide how to respond to a message from a friend of mine."

Most people do not understand what it is to be a scientist. They assume you must work in a lab or at the keyboard of a supercomputer. Neither of these things is necessary. People think being a scientist must involve chemical reactions and beakers, or DNA, or lab rats, or radiation sources. Scientists must study earthquakes or brain waves or galaxies, or those odd life forms that thrive on deep-sea vents. Scientists collide particles, scientists mutate enzymes, scientists scatter neutrons.

But even for me, science is not about polymers and colloids. To say science is about reasoning would be part of it. Ultimately, science is just observing the world—all the world—accurately and not drawing any conclusions that cannot be supported. In summary, scientists are trained to detect bullshit. And the most nefarious bullshit out there—the bullshit that is the toughest to detect, the bullshit that is the toughest to expose—is always your own. When I first learned to operate an atomic force microscope, the postdoc teaching me to use the instrument warned me about some of the problems with AFM imaging. He said that when using an AFM, the many potential artifacts in the image allow you to see whatever it is you are expecting to see, unless you continually check yourself. In life, too, artifacts abound and distort our view. We can always set the rules to give us the outcome that affirms our preconceived beliefs. I am no better than most. Yes, I messed around with young guys because I believed the messing around could never turn into a relationship. And, yes, this blinded me to the person in my life with whom a lasting relationship may again be possible.

14

ONE CAN NOT HELP but have an ambivalent attitude towards Los Angeles. I have had great loves and great friendships in this city, but whenever I spend time in the leafy, cool Pacific Northwest or on California's Central Coast, I imagine my life might be better lived there, away from the Southland. My excitement when landing in Los Angeles, however, is like nowhere else on earth. Night landings are the best, awed by the expansive carpet of lights. Even when I touch down in daylight, like today, I stare out the window like a kid, trying to pick out landmarks as we sweep across the basin: my building downtown, campus, the neighborhood where I was raised. I know during these homecomings that despite the traffic and the poor urban planning, despite the smog, despite the feelings of isolation that creep in between weekends, despite everything, I belong here.

I ride the metro home and feel relieved to be surrounded by

English and Spanish. The heat leaving the station makes me sweat. My apartment is stuffy, so I turn on the air conditioner and hope it will be more comfortable when I return. A note from CJ welcoming me home sits atop the pile of mail on my kitchen counter. This friendship, too, does not appear to have been harmed irreparably. I look in the mirror; my face is stubbly and my hair unkempt. I think I smell. I leave anyway.

My car starts on the first try. Late afternoon congestion makes the drive to Silver Lake almost impossible. Exhausted, I turn off the radio to help me focus.

I knock on Russ's door and am simultaneously relieved and horror-struck when he answers it. He steps out on the porch, and we just look at each other.

"I'm such a fucking idiot," I say.

"Indeed," agrees Russ, "you are."

"I couldn't just email you back. I had to talk to you in person."

We stand silently a little longer. I twitch a little with fatigue and stare at the house next door.

"Maybe," Russ finally says, "maybe I should have said something sooner. I could not bear you moving on without me. Shit, Damon. I was worried about being able to face you and keep myself together, and you are the one starting to cry. Don't get me started."

"I wouldn't show up like this if I felt like moving on without you." I sniffle a little and wipe my face with my sleeve. "I haven't really slept for a couple of days, I'm permeated with stale airplane air, my stomach is raw with coffee, but I had to see you. I know apologies can only fix so much, but I want to be your boyfriend if you will still have me. I think I can finally do that well."

"It is OK." He grabs my elbow and squeezes it. "Of course I still want you to be my boyfriend." Russ's manner towards me finally softens.

"Maybe," I say, "I could get cleaned up and sleep and we could talk tomorrow."

"I am not letting you drive like this."

"It is OK. Traffic is going to die down. I don't have to work until Monday."

"I have a shower, Damon, and I have a razor and a toothbrush you can use. I'll make you something to eat while you get cleaned up. I'll throw these clothes in the wash, and you can sleep in my bed. Come inside—I'd kiss you, but you are really gross. You need to get cleaned up."

After I shower, I put a towel around my waist. Since I am not sure if either of Russ's roommates is home and I don't want to wander around the house like this, I just stay in Russ's bedroom. A June breeze blows bougainvillea blossoms through the open window and rolls them across the floor. Their festive crimson color makes me think of them as little paper lanterns. I stand at the window and watch people below walking their dogs around the perimeter of the reservoir. It is twilight. A Belle and Sebastian song plays quietly on the stereo. I look over and notice that it is not a CD, but the pirate radio station, on the air a little earlier than usual.

Russ brings a plate with two sandwiches and a couple glasses of lemonade and lets me choose if I want the roast beef sandwich or the turkey. He fetches a bag of potato chips, and then we sit on his floor and eat our meal.

"I need to say this, Damon. You can stay no matter what tonight, but if you want to be my boyfriend, you can only be with me. Nobody else."

I start to tell him that I already understood that, but instead I promise to love nobody but him. I tell him how important a friend he has been this past year, and that if I haven't thought of him as anything more, it was my own terribly narrow vision. I tell him how I had a crush on him from the start and how frantic I became leaving Budapest when I thought I had lost my chance with him, and I apologize again for being so oblivious.

"OK," I say, "I know this might sound funny, but would you be my date for Ron and Allan's commitment ceremony next month?"

"Certainly," he says.

After the sandwiches and the talking, Russ undresses and gets into bed with me. It eventually becomes dark, and by then we are just cuddling. Wrapped in Russ's arms, in evening's coolness, I feel we have retreated together into an ancient, sacred center. I stay awake as long as I can. The last thing I remember before sleeping is his barely parted lips kissing my shoulder so very softly.

Acknowledgments

Although I began this book before I met Robert Reincke, I am not sure that I could have finished it without him. I thank him for his love and inspiration. I would also like to thank John Reeder for his careful reading of this book.

Readings

A History of Hungary by László Kontler (New York: Palgrave, 2002)

The Hungarians by Paul Lendvai (Princeton: Princeton University Press, 2003)

Black Lamb and Grey Falcon by Rebecca West (New York: The Viking Press, 1943)